DATE DUE

DEMCO, INC. 38-2931

2. Overdue fees will be levied on all magazines,
   books, and phonograph record albums according
   to the schedule posted at the main desk.

3. DAMAGES AND LOSSES of Library-owned
   property will be paid for by the borrower.

4. RESPONSIBILITY for all books taken on his
   card rests with the borrower as well as for all
   fees accruing to his card. Notification of loss
   of card does not free the borrower of his responsibility.

PRINTED IN U.S.A.

Cynthia

By E. V. Cunningham

CYNTHIA

SAMANTHA

SALLY

MARGIE

HELEN

PENELOPE

LYDIA

SYLVIA

PHYLLIS

ALICE

SHIRLEY

Cynthia

• • • • • • • • •

A NOVEL BY
E. V. Cunningham, *pseud.*
Howard Melvin Fast

New York   1968

William Morrow & Company, Inc.

For Judy
she knows why

Cynthia

Chapter 1

Alex Hunter, my boss, admires consistency. No one has ever accused him of inconsistency; he is unpleasant when he wants to be and he is also unpleasant when he desires to be pleasant. It has been rumored that somewhere he has wife and children. I don't envy them. He is my boss because he heads the investigatory department of the third largest insurance company in the world, and I continue to work for him because when he fires me the people upstairs talk to him and mollify him, and because I have to pay my rent and my alimony, but mostly my alimony. He is in his late fifties and gray and sour, and he has a cop mentality.

He greeted me with his usual distaste on this early March morning and made his comment upon the weather. "March is a lousy month," he said.

I recognized it as a friendly exploratory remark, and I knew that he wanted something that amounted to money. I had no inkling as to what it was. No big jewel hauls lately, no yachts stolen, no Picassos sneaked out of museums—I put on my bemused, innocent, open boyish expression, and said cheerfully, "Good morning, Mr. Hunt. Yes, indeed, sir, March weather here in New York is quite inclement."

"Harvey, why do I always end up disliking you when I try to be pleasant? Sit down."

"You dislike my integrity and independence," I said. "You envy my freedom."

"Your freedom is an illusion," he said coldly. "Your wife is trying to attach your wages. Sit down. You bilked this company out of a finder's fee of fifty grand on the Sabin case and you blew it in the past six months."

"Just recollect that I split it with Miss Cotter," I said indignantly. "As you know, she was the kid who took the hard end of the Sabin case. She deserved as much credit as I did. Then the government took its bite. Did it ever occur to you to work for Internal Revenue, Mr. Hunter, sir?"

"All right, Harvey—"

"I was also eight thousand dollars in debt, including back alimony, but that is none of your Goddamn business, Mr. Hunter, and anyway you give me—"

"Don't say it, Harvey," he interrupted. "Don't force anything. We got a relationship, for what it is. Don't make it impossible. This is a big job—do you want to listen or do you want to quit?"

"I want to quit, but I'll listen."

"All right. Now sit down."

I sat down facing him, attempting to compose a facial expression that combined bright intelligence and controlled dislike. It was not easy.

"Today is Thursday," Hunter said. He always sounds most important when he is proposing the obvious.

"Yes, sir."

"On Monday," he continued, "Cynthia Brandon walked

[8]

out of her father's twenty-two-room Park Avenue apartment and disappeared. Today is Thursday. No sign of her. No word."

"I live in a room and a half. I don't believe there is a twenty-two-room flat in this town."

"Believe it, Harvey. There are lots of them, and this one is at 626 Park Avenue, and when we finish with our business, I'll call the owners and have them furnish a floor plan for your social edification."

"You can be very funny."

"I am only trying to keep my temper, Harvey. As I said, Cynthia Brandon walked out of her father's apartment on Monday and vanished. Do you know who she is?"

"No."

"Good. You are ignorant but honest, Harvey. Have you heard of E.C. Brandon—Elmer Cantwell Brandon?"

"Private bankers—*Gerson and Brandon?*"

"Good, Harvey. Very good."

"Millionaire?"

"Oh, many millions, Harvey. Maybe billions—who counts?"

"Wife—Alice Brandon one kid?" I ventured.

"Right you are. See, just takes a little prodding."

I hated him quietly, coldly and efficiently and made up my mind not to rise to his bait. I decided to play it out and then hit him in the only way I knew how to hit Hunter—with a price.

"The girl's gone," I said.

"Right, Harvey. The girl is gone. Now just listen to this—we carry all of E.C. Brandon's insurance, every nickel of it, and we also underwrite the various insurance needs of *Gerson and Brandon*. We just happen to carry two policies on

[9]

the kid—that is, on Miss Cynthia Brandon. We insure her against kidnapping for one million dollars, and we also insure her life for a second million dollars. E.C. owns both policies. Two million dollars, Harvey—two million sweet, green dollars."

"I don't believe it."

"No?" Hunter smiled sweetly. "Why don't you believe it?"

"Because no company is that stupid."

"We're that stupid, Harvey. Do you know what our annual billing to *Gerson and Brandon* is? Including personal items by partners and employees, the premiums amount to over two hundred thousand dollars a year—including property, of course. That is very nice business, Harvey, just as the insurance business is nice business and can thereby afford to pay wages to people like yourself. So if E.C. Brandon desires a couple of curious policies and is willing to pay top dollar for premiums, we write those policies."

"Kidnapping? Is that common?"

"It's hard to say, because when companies write these offbeat policies they don't put them into statistics. They are usually written as a favor to someone, and any public exposure reduces confidence in the company. What good would it do Prudential, for example, to publicize the fact that they have insured Mrs. Uppidedup's pet poodle for twenty grand? Not that they ever did, Harvey—I am merely making a case in point. But every company does these things."

"But the life insurance—how does that connect? You say Brandon owns the policies. But who is the beneficiary?"

"Brandon."

"What? You said he was as rich as Rockefeller."

"More or less, Harvey, more or less. He likes money. I never met him, but presumably he likes money more than he likes his daughter. That is why he is bugged by this kidnapping thing. Also, my dear boy, since he owns the policy, he comes into a million dollars tax-free. You don't laugh at a million dollars tax-free."

I laughed. I had to laugh, and one day Alex Hunter, who is built like a five-foot, eight-inch gorilla, will do his best to make me stop laughing. He will succeed too, notwithstanding the fact that I have better than twenty years on him.

"You laugh at it," Hunter said. With great control, he continued, "However, this company faces the possibility of a million payout if the girl is kidnapped or dead, and two million dollars if she is both."

"You mean she's been kidnapped?"

"Did I say that? I said she walked out and has not been heard from. There is no indication that she's been kidnapped —except E.C. Brandon's fixation on kidnapping and his very neurotic fear that this is just what has happened."

"You said he liked money more than girls, so what's his beef? He's covered, isn't he?"

"He's covered for a million dollars of our money, Harvey. But suppose the girl is kidnapped and they touch him for two million or five million? Now that puts him in a most difficult position, doesn't it? Even you can see that, Harvey."

"You mean that if he refuses to pay and sells the girl down the river, the odor commences?"

"Exactly, Harvey. Maybe no girl is worth two million but the public is sentimental."

"That's his worry, isn't it?"

"No, Harvey—oh, no. It's our worry. You see, he wants to increase the kidnap insurance—double it. Two million dollars. That is how we know, Harvey. You see, we asked about the girl and upstairs they wanted to talk to her. No girl. She has been missing four days."

"Then tell him to go soak his head."

[11]

"No, Harvey. If it were you with a lousy little policy on your life, we would be happy to tell you to go soak your head. But not E.C. Brandon. Do you remember how much his business amounts to?"

"I remember."

"So we don't tell him to go soak his head, Harvey."

"No. But Goddamn it, I just don't believe in million dollar payoffs. How?"

"Harvey, Harvey—the world moves and you let it pass you by. If the girl has been kidnapped, she could be in Africa, while instructions come from Brazil for E.C. to put the money in a numbered Swiss account. There are ways, I assure you."

"And you mean that you are going to double his policy?"

"Yes."

"Is the other laid off?"

"Harvey, we are not a betting parlor. We are the third largest insurance company in the world and we carry our own reinsurance. That makes not one damn bit of difference. The company is in for two million and may be in for three. Whatever we do in the bookkeeping department, money is money."

"The cops?"

"No! That's emphatic—from E.C. Brandon's point of view, and just between us, from ours. No cops at this point."

"Which leaves me where?" I asked him.

"Oh, come off it, Harvey. You know damn well what I want. I want you to find the girl. If she has been kidnapped, pay off the kidnappers. If she's alive, bring her back. If she's dead, pin down the fact. That will cost us one million providing you can also prove she had never been kidnapped."

"You're all heart, Mr. Hunter."

[12]

"And I'll ignore that one too—for the moment, Harvey."

"I meant it both ways," I said. "You pay me a couple of yards a week and pickings—"

"You call the twenty-five grand on the Sabin case pickings?"

"Pickings. I waited a long time for that. A plumber earns more than I do, and you don't want anything at all, do you? Oh, no sir, Mr. Hunter, not at all. Only, 'Harvey, my boy, go out and find the girl and if she's kidnapped pay them off and if she's dead, get a death certificate.' Just little Harvey Krim, Boy Scout. You got sixteen operatives working for you and one hundred and eleven investigators—but this is just you and Harvey, your buddy boy, face to face, no cops, no private agencies, just Harvey."

I watched him through that long address, and while one of his eyelids twitched a bit, he never lost his temper and he never got mad—and it doesn't take much to make Alex Hunter mad. So I knew I was in, and if it was an idiot, impossible job, there would be a lot of idiot impossible dollar bills to go with it.

"This is a very delicate thing, Harvey—you know that."

"You mean I am playing footsie with law and order every step of the way."

"I never said that."

"You said pay off the kidnappers, didn't you?"

"Just between you and me, Harvey, I don't think the girl was abducted or kidnapped or even harmed. I just think she had a bellyful of the old man and walked out."

"Then why don't you leave it alone?"

"Because a possible pay out of three million dollars demands action, not indifference or luck."

"How old is the kid?"

[13]

"Twenty."

"College?"

"Two and a half years. Then she quit."

"Lived at home?"

"Since January—when she quit college."

"Suppose I have to pay off—how?"

"With cash."

"How much?"

"As much or as little as you can buy out with. You make a price. The more you save, the better the company likes you."

"It's no good unless I have the money."

Hunter observed me thoughtfully, his eyes narrowing. "All right, Harvey, what do you mean—you have the money?"

"This is what I mean. If the money is to serve any purpose, I need it when I need it, immediately. A payoff isn't tomorrow or when the check clears. It's now—right this minute."

"And how much money were you thinking about, Harvey?"

"A bird in the hand, that's all," I said. One million, two million—those are phone numbers. A hundred grand in a briefcase—that is real money, real, solid negotiable money."

Hunter thought about this for a while, while his cold blue eyes measured me with simple intent to kill, and then he said, "If I read you right, Harvey, you expect us to give you a bright, shiny new briefcase containing one hundred thousand dollars. Am I correct?"

"More or less."

"And how do you account for the money, Harvey?"

"I don't."

"No?"

"No."

"Go soak your head, Harvey."

"You see, Mr. Hunter, if I buy her out, I buy her out. If I simply bring her home, the money is not used. And if she's dead, the money is not used either. For two months now, Mr. Hunter, you've had me scrounging around after petty fur frauds and phony jewel losses, and I'm ready to tell you to shove it all. I don't like working for you and I don't like you."

"Well, Harvey!"

"Nuts, Mr. Hunter! You give me one swift pain. Why the hell don't you fire me? Why don't you work me over, like you're aching to do, just like you keep seeing on TV, only you think you could do it better?"

"Why do you think, Harvey?"

"I'll tell you why. Because they told you upstairs that either you produce or you're finished, that's why. Because E.C. Brandon told you that if one word of this gets into the papers, he washes his hands of this company. And because the only kind of man you hire for the lousy wages you pay are poor stupid slobs who take what you dish out—myself included. But now I've got you up against the wall."

Hunter smiled thinly and said to me, "You're a remarkable bastard Harvey. What's on your mind?"

"Money."

"Spell it out."

"I'll gamble on this one. I want the hundred thousand dollars, and I'll handle the payout, and what's left over is mine."

"And suppose there's no kidnapping. Suppose the girl just took it into her head to get out."

"Likely enough."

"You get the hundred grand?"

"Yes."

"Go to hell, Harvey."

I stood up and asked whether that meant I was fired?

"They fire and hire you upstairs now, Harvey. You're their white-haired boy. Suppose she was kidnapped and the kidnappers want more than you got?"

"I come back to you."

"I hope they fire you, Harvey," Hunter said. "You're snotty and preposterous, and I don't even think you're very smart."

I went back to my own office and wondered whether I had blown the whole thing. It was too iffy—too open-ended.

"What is it, wonder boy?" Mazie Gilman, our chief researcher, asked me. "What eats at your poor, shriveled soul?"

She shares an office with Harry Hopkins—another investigator—and me, and she is middle-aged, overweight and sort of ugly, and she knows everything in the world. I asked about E.C. Brandon.

"He has more money than Rockefeller."

"Everyone's an authority on Rockefeller's bank account."

"I didn't know you were a Republican, Harvey. Brandon is Texas-rich. His father was the Brandon of Brandon Oil. He was shipped off to Harvard, and he subsequently made his headquarters on Wall Street. But he still has a finger in Texas pies. We have a pretty solid Texas business through him, and you know what it means for any New York insurance firm to buck that Dallas crowd. They are out for our scalp, but the old Brandon wealth is West Texas, and they have no great love for the brand new Dallas insurance kings. Still, it's pretty shaky."

"You got a big mouth and I love you," I said; and then the phone on my desk rang. It was Smedly from upstairs. Smedly is one of the more important vice-presidents, in charge of personnel, and he speaks softly and takes a fatherly tone, and now he spoke gently about what a shame it was that Alex Hunter and I don't get along, when each of us in his own way was a rare and sterling character. Perhaps if he and I had a chat—that is, Smedly and I—we could smooth over some rough edges. This was not new. We had had our chats in the past. I went upstairs.

Smedly smiled at me. He was a middle-sized man, with steel-rimmed glasses and gray hair, and he had that same look of intangible efficiency that seems to permeate everyone in the insurance business. He began by informing me that I had often been the subject of discussion at personnel meetings.

"You have so many obvious talents, Mr. Krim—intelligence, originality—and virtues like independence, good, old-fashioned virtues—" (He mentioned no other virtues.) "—but there is a streak of intolerance in your nature that makes us pass over you whenever you are obviously a candidate for promotion."

"Intolerance? Good God, Mr. Smedly, as far as the civil rights movement is concerned—"

"I don't mean that, Mr. Krim. Toleration is a two-edged sword."

"You mean tolerance, don't you, Mr. Smedly?" I couldn't resist that, and if you want my life story, that spells it out.

"There's no difference, is there, Mr. Krim?" Smedly asked, the blue eyes behind the steel-rimmed glasses narrowing a bit.

"Well, you see, toleration means to endure someone. Tolerance means to respect them."

"Thank you, Mr. Krim." He was straining for the fatherly tone at this point. "I sometimes wonder, Mr. Krim, why you reject the social amenities. We operate as a team here, but you consistently refuse to become a functioning part of the team. That is what I meant by tolerance," he said carefully. "I meant your tolerance for us, our needs, our ways. Now take this Brandon case. The company calls upon you because it faces a serious loss—oh, yes indeed, a payout of over a million dollars is a bitter pill for any company to swallow. We have faith in you. We feel that you could find this girl; we even feel that if, God forbid, she has been abducted, you might deal with the abductors in such a manner as to ensure the child's safety. That is our primary interest, Mr. Krim, the child's safety. You know that in any case like this, we are willing to pay necessary expenses—but when you ask for a hundred thousand dollars with no strings attached, you certainly give me the feeling of a profound lack of respect."

"What is disrespectful about a hundred grand?"

"Perhaps a better word is preposterous."

"Then why bring it up at all?" I demanded, unable to conceal my irritation. "You know what you want me to do. How do I do it? Why don't you be realistic? Suppose the girl was grabbed? Who does a job like that? Crumbs, psychopaths, hopheads—the organized people don't go in for that kind of thing. The only way I know is to buy and pay, and not to have to account for the money. That's why I specify that I want my fee out of that money. I don't want any accusations of bilking the company."

"Ridiculous!" The fatherly tone was gone now.

"It's a lousy three percent."

"There is a limit to our patience, Krim."

"Why?" I asked him. "We could go back to that virtue you reminded me about before. Independence. I am independent as hell. I have an offer to teach Criminology at the University of North Carolina. So fire me."

[18]

"Why don't you cool down," Smedly said. "What the devil do you know about criminology?"

Then we both grinned. I never knew that Smedly had it in him, but there it was—an honest, open, comprehending grin.

"Suppose the girl turns up tomorrow?" he asked me.

I shrugged.

"All right, Harvey," he said, calling me by my first name—as good a way as any of stating that we were down to realities. "You will not undertake this without a fat fee. You work for us, but you invite me to fire you. The alternative is to buy you. Do I state the case properly?"

"Just about."

"How would you describe your services?"

"As far as I know, I am the best insurance investigator around. Maybe in the country. If there's anyone better, I haven't met him."

"Also the most unscrupulous."

"I still hold a license."

"Ten thousand dollars fee. The rest is returnable—ninety thousand dollars of working capital."

"Twenty."

"Fifteen, Harvey. Not a nickel more. Eighty-five thousand dollars returnable."

"Without papers. On my word."

"All right. You are one of the most unscrupulous bastards I have ever known, Mr. Krim, but I believe you are honest."

"Thank you."

"How do you want it?"

"Two certified checks. The fifteen is income. The eighty-five remains company money in work."

"All right." He flicked on the intercom over his highly polished, old-fashioned desk, and ordered the checks drawn.

[19]

Then he leaned back, put the tips of his fingers together, observed me over his glasses, and finally asked me,

"Just how much has Alex Hunter told you about this, Harvey? By the way, I shall call you Harvey from here on. I think the situation demands it, don't you?"

"By all means. Hunter sort of filled me in on Brandon and his daughter."

"Did he tell you what his yearly premiums amount to?"

"A couple of hundred thousand?"

"Nonsense!" he snorted. "A damn sight more. Never mind how much—but enough to force us to double the coverage on the girl. I don't want to give you a lecture on money, Harvey, and anyway I suspect that you know as much about its symbolic side as I do. Brandon is a money man. All other gods are gone. Only money."

"What is he worth—Brandon?"

"Who the devil knows, Harvey?—well, maybe the devil does. At his level, it is not what a man is worth in the old-fashioned sense, no dollar count. What are his resources? What can he command if the need arises? Who knows— maybe a billion, maybe half of that—but very big, Harvey."

"I am impressed."

"You damn well are. Now, Harvey, listen to me." He leaned toward me over the shiny mahogany desk and tapped upon it with a well-manicured forefinger. "I am no Alex Hunter. You are not dealing with boobs or cops. You are dealing with Homer Smedly, born fifty-five years ago in Akron, Ohio, and today the vice-president of the third largest insurance company in the world. I know something about you, so it is only fitting that you know something about me. You pulled off a brilliant coup in the Sabin Case, and I believe you have intelligence. It is not the kind of intelligence I would ever hire for anything except your line of work, but I respect it because any kind of intelligence is in extremely short supply. I am going to hand you two checks in a few minutes—checks so preposterous in kind and cause that they will constitute a major headache for my comptroller. I hand them over to you without complaint. In return, Harvey, I want Cynthia Brandon. I want her alive—and God help you if you don't deliver."

"Suppose she's dead already?"

"You should have thought of that before, Harvey."

"God help me? What does that mean?"

"I leave it up to your imagination, saying only that you will wish you had never been born. I am a very powerful man, Harvey, and far more dangerous than someone like Alex Hunter."

"I realize that," I said cheerfully. But I was not feeling cheerful—not by any means.

"You can throw in your cards, Harvey. Drop the job. Then you're fired, which is a comparatively painless process. Walk through that door and that's the end of it."

"No, sir, Mr. Homer Smedly," I said. "Fifteen thousand dollars is a lot of money, and I will do a lot of things for it—even incur your wrath. So I am on the Brandon case."

"Good. Then sit down over there and wait for the checks. I am a busy man, Harvey, and I have work to do."

Chapter 2

I remember taking an intelligence test when I was pretty much of a kid, and one of the questions showed a diagram of a fenced field. The proposition was that this field was covered with high grass and that a ball had been thrown into it and currently was lying hidden in the grass. Problem: using a pencil line to describe your movements, show how you would go about finding the ball.

I could not have more than twelve or thirteen at the time, but I knew what they wanted. They wanted a geometric crosshatch that would cover every inch of the field; but I also knew that human beings do not function that way. If a machine had lost the ball and another machine had set about to find it, the crosshatch gridiron would have been perfectly proper. A man—even a sensible man—would wander around, kicking at the grass, thinking, trying to remember the direction of the ball when it crossed the fence, trying to gauge whether it had bounced or not. The pencil line of his movements would have amounted to a meaningless, sort of idiotic scrawl.

It's a good description of how I work—in a sort of senseless scrawl that makes sense to me and not to anyone else; and thereby they have me on the books as a smart investigator. But all I do is kick at the grass until something turns up.

Along with that, sometimes, I have a gleam of a notion; but nothing to boast about; and if I do have even a flicker of a dream, I call Lucille Dempsey, who is assistant to the chief librarian in the Donnell Branch of the New York Public Library. The said branch is located on 53rd Street, between Fifth and Sixth Avenue, directly facing the Museum of Modern Art, which up until recently served the best cheap lunch in New York for one dollar. Even when their lunch took a large jump in price, it remained the best for the money in that part of town.

Today, however, when I telephoned Lucille, she asked acidly whether I proposed to meet the raised museum prices once again. I told her no, rather severely, and proposed that she lunch with me at the Woman's Exchange on Madison Avenue and 54th.

"Harvey—you are not for real. Never."

"So I have some neurotic problems."

"Harvey, you're simply chintzy. You're the very last of the big spenders and it's an illness with you."

"What is wrong with the Woman's Exchange?"

"Nothing, Harvey. It's a delightful place and it has the best food in town and it's marvelously inexpensive. Just once, please, take me to a bad restaurant that costs more than a dollar-eighty for a lunch. I'll take the check myself. Of course I am not angry with you, Harvey."

I went to the bank first, and walking there, I thought about Lucille. Being as nervous as the next man in New York, I once decided that what I needed more than anything else in the world was psychoanalysis, and I put in eleven

[24]

months with Dr. Fred Bronstein on East 75th Street. In the course of this, I talked about Lucille Dempsey—a thing I remember very well, since it came after eleven months of futility.

"Doc," I said to him on that particular morning, "there is this girl called Lucille Dempsey."

"Go on," he said in that quiet, offhand way of his—the tone he always used when he had a hand around his sharpest knife, ready to draw it and plunge it into your mental guts.

"She is twenty-nine years old and five feet-seven inches tall, honey-colored hair, brown eyes and just quietly intelligent. She comes from Western Massachusetts and she works in the Donnel Branch of the New York Public Library and she is a Radcliffe graduate. She's a Presbyterian but hardly works at it, and she has been fond of me for a long time for reasons I don't understand, and she wants me to marry her."

There was silence after that, and I waited out a decent period of time and then asked him, "Well?"

"Well?"

"Well, Goddamnit, aren't you going to say something?"

"What should I say, Harvey? You're a nut. My role here is to listen, not to comment."

"That's a hell of a thing for a responsible doctor to say!"

"It sure is, Harvey."

I paid him cash. He wanted to send me a bill, but I paid him cash right there and never went back. I thought about it now, walking to the bank. Now and then I missed Dr. Bronstein.

When I have dealings at the bank more important than depositing my paycheck in time to cover my alimony, I deal with one of the younger officers, whose name is Frank Vancleffin. He is at least two years younger than I am and he looks up to me. He sits at the other side of half an acre of terrazzo floors and marble counters, and he always watches my approach with pleasure. This time, when I laid down the two checks, he was duly impressed.

"That's a lot of money, Mr. Krim," he said approvingly.

"Only the small one's for deposit."

"You know, Mr. Krim," he said, "it's very interesting to deal with people who call a check for fifteen thousand dollars small. But I guess as a private eye, lots of these things—I mean these kind of situations—come your way."

"I am not a private eye. I'm only an insurance investigator, Mr. Vancleffin."

"I tell my kids you're a private eye. You don't mind that, do you?"

"Oh, no. No. Not at all."

"I also tell them you carry a gun."

"I don't."

"No?"

"No," I said apologetically. "You see, I know a lot of cops, and they would feel very uneasy if I had a gun, and even if I had a permit, they would probably try to get it away from me."

"Because you might shoot some innocent person?"

"Myself."

"You?"

"Right."

"How would I tell that to the kids? You're putting me on."

"Maybe a little."

"It's all right if I tell the kids about the big one—the eighty-five thousand?"

"No reason why not."

[26]

"And you're sure you want it all in traveler's checks?"

"Five ten thousand dollar checks, five five thousand, and ten of one thousand each."

"It makes a tidy little package, Mr. Krim."

"Yes, indeed."

"Well, I'm just the banker."

But I was a few minutes late for my lunch date with Lucille Dempsey, because I had to wait until they had called the company and made certain that my honest face had an honest pair of hands to tag along with it. She had snagged the last remaining table at the Woman's Exchange, and when I sat down opposite her, she said, "For heaven's sake, Harvey, you look as smug and foolish as a Cheshire cat. Is it your birthday?"

"No, but I just deposited fifteen thousand dollars to the account of Harvey L. Krim."

"And it's yours, Harvey?"

"Absolutely—after I put five away for the tax and then try to make a deal with the woman I was once married to. I figure to offer her eight thousand dollars cash to let me off the hook. I hear she's in love with some feller, so she may just take it. That leaves us two thousand to get married on and have a honeymoon in the Canary Islands and to get one of those see-through apartments on Third Avenue."

"You're out of your mind, Harvey. Let's order some food."

While we waited for the food and while we ate, I told her the story of Cynthia Brandon and the hundred thousand dollars.

"I don't believe it," she said constructively, when I had finished. "I just don't believe it, Harvey."

I showed her the traveler's checks, eighty-five thousand in one tight little black folder.

[27]

"Well, I still don't believe it, but why on earth do you want it in traveler's checks?"

"So I can carry it around with me. How else could you keep eighty-five thousand dollars of real money in your pocket?"

"But why?"

We were at the dessert, which is the best dessert in New York, and mine was ice cream. I ate it carefully and gratefully, while she watched me with despair.

"You know, I often think the world is crumbling," she said, "I mean compared to the way it was when I was a kid, Harvey, but it can't get so crumbly that the third largest insurance company in the country gives you eighty-five thousand dollars, but you don't know why or what you are going to do with it? Or do you?"

"No."

"Then it doesn't make sense."

"No. I asked you to marry me—or don't you remember?"

"I remember, Harvey. I remember that you asked the Cotter girl to marry you, and don't you think I have as much sense as she had?"

"I think you have more sense than any girl I ever knew. I think that's what's the trouble with you. And it's only because you have so much sense that I expect you to come up with an answer."

"Harvey, what on earth are you talking about? What answer?"

"Cynthia."

I paid the check and we went outside and I walked her back to the library, and in the course of it she mentioned my qualities. Lucille doesn't praise me, although she thinks she does, and she referred to the fact that instead of doing any-

[28]

thing creative or admirable, I was a shamus for an oversize legal bookie; although she doesn't use words like shamus, and I often think myself that such words are more gauche than definitive, she has no great admiration for the insurance business, particularly because she blames them for my own deterioration.

"Is that really how you go about solving a case, Harvey?" she asked me.

"Sort of."

"And you expect me to come up with Cynthia?"

"Oh, no—just some notion about her."

"And you're serious?"

"You're damn right."

"Well, then you're crazy," she said.

"No. You'll see."

"You mean just out of the clear sky I will call you up and say, 'Harvey, I know where you can find Cynthia?' "

"Maybe not just that way. But almost."

"Hah!" she said.

Chapter 3

The building at 626 Park Avenue, which spreads itself over half a city block, rises up twenty-nine stories and contains forty-three apartments. According to one of those statistical studies which our company adores—believing along with Mark Twain that there are lies, damn lies and statistics—the combined wealth of the inmates of 626 Park Avenue is slightly under a billion dollars; which explains why it is only Fort Knox that is harder to bust into. However, since we write something like five or six million dollars worth of personal property insurance in the building, the doorman is no stranger to me. He is a large, fleshy, crafty product of Flatbush, who goes by the name of Homer Clapp, and his mental equipment for the job is a sort of animal-like suspicion of anything under a million dollars.

He held out a hand automatically, and I put fifty cents in it and told him that I was on my way up to interview E.C. Brandon.

"You're breaking your heart, Harvey," he nodded, regarding the money in his palm. "You know, I can return this to you on a loan basis. I don't even charge no interest, and you can buy subway tokens."

"Drop dead."

"Anyway, Brandon is not home. His wife is there."

I put a whole dollar in his hand. "Have you seen the daughter lately?"

"Nope."

"Since when?"

"Maybe last week. You sure you're all right?" folding the dollar carefully into his pocket.

"Can you remember anything about when you last saw her?"

"I seen her—period. What's special?"

"That's what I would like to know. What was she wearing?"

"Clothes," he explained, and then I persuaded him to call Mrs. Brandon and ask her, please would she be so kind as to see Mr. Krim from the insurance company. Mrs. Brandon must have been bored, because she said that she would be delighted.

I have been in posh apartments here and there on New York's East Side, so I am not easily impressed. The Brandon place impressed me. A butler opened the door for me, and I looked out across half an acre of marble foyer, not big enough for tennis but perfectly all right for badminton. The badminton effect was heightened by a pair of curved staircases which swept up to the balcony of the duplex, leaving the ceiling of the entranceway some twenty-two feet high, like a set from *Gone With the Wind* transported to Park Avenue and Sixty-fifth Street. As the butler took my topcoat, what was evidently Mrs. Brandon appeared at the top of the lefthand staircase, posed a moment, and then descended. She was dressed in lavender, the color of the wallpaper. The side-chairs in the entranceway were upholstered in a sort of magenta, and the butler wore a mauve cummerbund.

"Dear Mr. Krim!" my hostess cried, leaning toward me as if she were about to kiss me but then remembering that we had not met before. "Dear Mr. Krim, how good of you to come!"

She had quite a breath. She was no vodka drinker; the load she had consumed surrounded her, and suddenly I was filled with respect for the fact that she walked quite steadily.

"Please come inside, Mr. Krim," she said with careful dignity. "Do you like Mallietti's work? He's called the Purple Queen. But I do think that is rather nasty, don't you? I mean a man's sex life should have absolutely no bearing upon his talents as an interior decorator—and don't you think Mallietti is the most precious in talent we have? I mean, don't you?"

"I am sure," I agreed.

The butler opened the door to a living room and then closed it behind us. The living room was about thirty by thirty, and the walls were covered with picture-paper scenes of French gardens done in various shades of lavender. Most of the furniture was white, and the floor was sheltered by an Aubusson carpet that probably cost no more than a hundred shares of IBM.

Mrs. Brandon steered herself across the room to an end table, which was decorated by a beautiful Chinese porcelain horse that was unhappily split in half. It was a sort of purple.

"It's not so much that the damn thing is broken," she said. "But it's the only one of its color. It really can't be repaired. And there's no other like it in the whole world. It's real T'ang, you know—sixth-century."

[33]

She handed the two pieces of the horse to me, and I looked at them carefully and with great interest.

"Not sixth-century," I said. "T'ang was 618 to 906, as nearly as they can date it, but this would be ninth-century, I think. It's the Bactrian horse, which the Mongols rode on their raids into China, and then, lost, strayed, stolen, captured, it bred as a Chinese animal. The very fine one at the Met here has the same red paint on the saddle."

"How wonderful!" She clapped her hands and applauded me. "You are clever, Mr. Krim. We must have a drink to celebrate. You know, Mallietti charged me eleven thousand dollars for it—and it's worth ten times that, don't you agree?"

"It would be if it were real, Mrs. Brandon," I told her. "There are maybe ten of these things in the whole world, and they are all glazed blue. This lavender thing is a fake and maybe not the best fake in the world. I think I could put my finger on the kiln in Italy where it was glazed and fired. It's good work, and it's worth sixty dollars in Bloomingdale's— but that's all."

She froze and then she unfroze. "How dare you, you crumby little bastard!" she exploded. "How dare you come in here and talk to me like that! I ought to toss you the hell out of here!" All through this, her expression of wan daintiness shrouded in purple never changed. The anger was of voice not of attitude, and then the voice dropped and she said, "The hell with it, Buster. Let's have a drink." She took the two pieces of the horse and dropped them into a waste basket. "What's yours? Do business with queens and you get what you deserve. Well, Jesus, don't just stand there, Buster —what do you want to drink?"

"I don't drink during working hours," I apologized.

"Well, wouldn't you know it! How do you want to cele-

brate the ten grand you just saved the company? Do you
mind if I have just a touch of gin and soda. I got gas—chronic.
I know it sounds like hell for a delicate lady in lavender to be
belching all over the place, but there it is. You don't mind if
I have one? Gas is the lousiest affliction a lady can have."

"Please."

She poured fluid into a glass, half-gin, half-seltzer, toasted
me and wanted to know how come I knew so much about
T'ang horses.

"You get a rounded knowledge in the insurance business,
but I'm not here about T'ang horses, Mrs. Brandon. If you
have a ten-thousand dollar specification on that piece of pot-
tery, my company will pay it without a whimper—much less
send a man over here to check it out. If you want me to, I'll
put in a memo to the fact that it broke in two. I don't have to
mention that it's a fake because they couldn't care less in the
Brandon account."

"You mean E.C. is good for that kind of business?"

"He certainly is, Mrs. Brandon."

"Just between you and me, Buster, how much is he
worth?"

"Anybody's guess—but the way they talk, he must have
more money than Fort Knox. Don't you know?"

"Me? Buster, day by day, I know less about E.C. Brandon."

"Shall I put in for the horse?"

"For the ten grand? What for, Buster? What can I do with
ten grand, drink it? That is, if I ever got my hands on it. If
E.C. ever found out that I had flimflammed him on ten thousand dollars, he would take me apart. He dreams about
money the way a hooker dreams about virginity. No—nothing
is a rescue mission. You are looking at a faded lavender flower
of forty-two—ah, nuts to that. I am forty-seven, Buster. I

[35]

made it. I married a rich man. And if you are not here for the filly, what brings you?"

"I thought maybe you'd bring it up."

"Bring what up?"

"Cynthia."

"Cynthia? What about Cynthia, bless her heart?"

"I hear she walked out."

She came up to me and kissed me lightly on the cheek. Except for the physical blow of alcoholic vapors, it was a sort of nice gesture, but I am hardly ever objective on the question of women. I like them, regardless of shape, height and age.

"Bless your heart, Buster," she said, "if you were E.C.'s daughter, wouldn't you walk out?"

"It's hard for me to think of myself as E.C.'s daughter, Mrs. Brandon, but maybe under the circumstances I would."

"Call me Alice. We are practically getting drunk together, and I begin to see through my lovely inebriated haze. E.C. has buzzed you on the kidnapping. You know, E.C. is a nut on the question of kidnapping. But what has that got to do with an insurance company?"

"He carries kidnapping insurance," I told her.

"No."

"It's a fact. And he also carries a nice bundle of life insurance on the girl."

"Oh? And who is the beneficiary?"

"He is. He also owns the policies."

"You know," she said thoughtfully, "he is a worse son of a bitch than I had imagined."

"Well, I don't know. He likes money."

"Who doesn't? But you don't think Cynthia has been kidnapped, Buster, do you?"

[36]

"Do you?"

"No. Cynthia got a dose too much of E.C. and walked out. She should have done that long ago. Only Cynthia has principles. I would have robbed him blind."

"You like Cynthia?"

"We got a common enemy."

"And where is he?"

"Who?"

"The enemy," I said.

"In his office. Presently, if the mood takes him, he returns here, looks at me with withering contempt—and so starts another lovely evening."

The door opened as she began to speak, and presently we both turned, and there he was, regarding us both with withering contempt. He wasn't bad-looking for his age and he kept in condition. He had a square jaw, a look of considered toughness, and if he had dyed his gray hair, he would have looked a good deal like Ronald Reagan. He had pale blue eyes which he fixed on me, demanding to know who I was and what I was doing there. I explained that my name was Harvey Krim—which never seems to impress anyone—and that I worked for the company that wrote his insurance.

"Then your business is with me and not with my wife," he said flatly.

"The last of the great gentlemen," Alice Brandon sighed. "Go with him, Buster. And drop in again—when we lose a diamond or an oil well or something."

"That will be quite enough, Alice," Brandon said.

Then she shut up. The ice in his voice was evidently a warning, and she took heed. I guessed that without the liquor, she was very afraid of him.

In his study, floor to ceiling with leatherbound books that

[37]

no one ever read and two chopped-out areas for ancestor portraits—Kennedy Galleries at a very good price—Brandon motioned for me to sit down. He then endeared himself to me by saying, "They told me they were putting their best man onto this. You don't look like anyone's best man. What did you say your name was?"

"Harvey Krim," I answered sweetly.

"Well, what do you propose to do about it?"

"About what?"

"Finding my daughter."

"I am told you believe that she's been kidnapped. Why?"

"She's been missing since Monday. Today is Thursday."

"Why kidnapped? Couldn't she walk out?"

"She tried that once. I told her that if it happened again, if twenty-four hours passed without her letting me know her exact whereabouts, I would cut her off without a penny."

"I see. She's the daughter of your former wife?"

"Exactly—which is neither here nor there."

"But if she were kidnapped—the note, the demand for money—the routine of kidnapping."

"They're biding their time."

"Still—"

"God damn it, Krim—I tell you she's been kidnapped! Do you know what it would do to my position right now if I had to come up with three, four million in cash?"

"But you are insured—"

"Don't be a horse's ass, Krim. This is going to be a large operation—"

"If she has been kidnapped—"

And so it went. He had her kidnapped and the ransom fixed at anywhere between five and ten million, and he could not be shaken from that position. I managed to get a few other facts about her, but it was hard to get him off the subject of the ransom.

Finally, I said to him, "Mr. Brandon, suppose I were to accept the proposition that your daughter has been kidnapped. Suppose you were asked to pay five million in ransom. Would you?"

He thought about it for a while, and then he said, "Smedly thought you would want some pictures." He handed me a little pile of pictures from his desk. One was in color, and it showed a head of red hair that must have come from her mother. She was a tall, long-legged, rangy kid, and while it doesn't exactly shine out of a picture, she seemed to have a mind of her own.

"Would you pay the ransom?" I asked again.

"What do you earn a week, Mr. Krim?" he asked, unable to keep an edge of contempt from his voice.

"I take home about two-sixty."

"Then you can hardly have any real relationship to a sum like five million dollars. To you, it's words. To me, it is reality."

"You haven't answered my question."

"In the market, Mr. Krim, you are not worth five million. I could buy a hundred better than you for five million. Why should it be any different with my daughter."

"Why indeed?" I could not help smiling a bit. "Still, it would be bad public relations, wouldn't it."

"It would. And before you grin at me like that again, Mr. Krim, I would ask you not only to remember that I have power in terms that money can buy—but that physically, I could break you in two."

"I will remember that," I said seriously. "No one wants to be broken in two, do they?"

[39]

"No, Mr. Krim."

"Meanwhile, it enlarges my knowledge to know that you are dangerous, Mr. Brandon. Shall I tell you something about myself?"

"Please do, Mr. Krim. I shall be pleasantly surprised to learn that you too are dangerous."

"No, I am not dangerous, Mr. Brandon. Not at all. But I am smart, which can be more worrisome."

"If you are smart, Mr. Krim, find my daughter."

"I may at that." I smiled and told him quickly, "I am not grinning, Mr. Brandon, so don't get ready to use your muscles. I am merely smiling with quiet satisfaction." Then I turned around and walked out of the room, and don't think it didn't take guts to do that. I half-expected him to slug me from behind, but he let me pass peacefully. It's funny how many men dream of themselves as big, persuasive punchers, and it's a little obscene, too. Only I hoped that I hadn't damaged the company's standing. After Smedly had been so nice to me, I would not want to cut down his score of fat premium payments.

The butler let me out. His name, according to the research sheet supplied to me by the company, was Jonas Biddle, but I am sure that was only a butler name and that he began life as Stanislaus Brunsky or something of the sort. Before he closed the door on me, I asked him, "Just how big a puncher is the master, old chap? Does he really haul off and take a shot at people who displease him? And how often?"

"Information has a price," he said softly.

"Go bite your hangnails," I told him. "You've been reading too much Mike Hammer."

"I don't read. I watch TV."

"Drop dead," I told him in a friendly manner. He did not take umbrage at hangnails but he knew all about dropping dead, and he slammed the door in my face. I took the elevator twenty-nine stories down and crossed the lobby to the dull afternoon haze, and there was a squad car from the nineteenth Precinct blocking the entrance and the big, youthful, handsome tweed-clad form of Sergeant Kelly awaiting me.

"Where do you buy your suits now?" I asked him.

"Brooks."

"You still look like a cop."

"Like hell I do. Harvey, tell me something—why do you always try to make it worse for yourself?"

"I don't try. It just comes naturally."

"Well, the Lieutenant wants to see you. You can ride over in the car or take a taxi or walk."

"Suppose I don't want to see the Lieutenant."

"Harvey, you want to see him."

"OK, I want to see him. I'll walk."

It had begun to snow, and it had been that way all day, snowing, pausing, snowing. March is a lousy month. Kelly walked with me and grumbled that he had always tried to like me.

"Everyone tries to like Harvey Krim," I agreed. "How did you know I was in there?"

"Where?"

"At 626 Park."

"A little bird told us."

"A lousy ratfink little bird of a doorman called Homer Clapp."

"Why be so bitter, Harvey?" Kelly said. "He's supposed to tell us. We haven't enough men to stake out the place. You know that."

"I pay him and he tells you."

Nor was our conversation any more enlightening as we walked to the precinct. The nineteenth Precinct is on 67th

[41]

Street, between Lexington and Third, an ancient, unwashed, red brick building that stands in the heart of the posh Silk Stocking district of Manhattan. Lieutenant Rothschild occupies a small room on the second floor of this building, where he sits behind a beat-up desk and sips milk for his ulcers and nurses his already substantial mistrust of the human species.

As I entered, he said to me unpleasantly, "Sit down, Harvey." And when I had placed myself gingerly upon a rickety, dusty chair, he continued, "You know, Harvey, a cop is a lot of things, day in and day out. He wants to be loved; we all want to be loved; but who loves him? You know what's worse than not being loved, Harvey?"

"Well—"

"Don't guess, Harvey. Worse than not being loved is to be made a patsy."

"I can understand that, Lieutenant," I agreed. "No one wants to be made a patsy."

"Good. I am glad you are so understanding, Harvey. We go out to catch crooks and put them in jail. You fence their merchandise and get the charges dropped. You make fools out of us every day of the week. You know what you do to my ulcers?"

"I'm sorry," I said.

"Like hell you are. What were you doing at 626 Park?"

"What is this, the Gestapo? Do I have to account for my movements to you?"

"No. Don't account for them. I'll make it so hot for you, you'll walk on blisters every step of the way."

"Lieutenant," I said gently, warmly, "why can't we be friends?"

"Because I don't want to be your friend, Harvey. I want to know what you were doing at 626."

"Seeing a friend?"

"No, Harvey. E.C. Brandon is no one's friend."

"That's the way it is with a cop. He's never going to admit that he knows anything. He's got to beat it out of you."

"Why were you seeing E.C. Brandon, Harvey?"

"He insures with the company."

"Harvey—listen to me." His eyes narrowed to thin slits, and his ulcers took over. "Now listen—you crap around with me on this one and I'll make it so hard for you—Goddamn you, Harvey, what in hell do you think the nineteenth Precinct is? We got more money sitting under our nose than practically all the rest of the world put together. That is no lark, Harvey. Now listen to me—where is the girl?"

"What girl?"

"Damn you. Cynthia Brandon. And never mind how I know that she's missing. Maybe cops are stupid—but not as stupid as you give them credit for being, Harvey. Where is she?"

"I don't know."

"Is that the truth?"

"It's the truth."

"All right. I am going to believe you—for the next ten minutes. Now what are you doing at Brandon's?"

"I told you. He insures with us."

"You told me nothing. I get more out of some crummy doorman than from you." Rothschild scowled and gulped his glass of milk. "So he insures with you. What's missing? What's been stolen? Why are you on the case?"

"Mrs. Brandon had a T'ang horse—or what presumed to be one. It turned out to be an Italian fake. It broke in two. I went around to look at it."

"Harvey, you're a liar!" Rothschild snapped. "Now, look—

[43]

I am coming to the point. Cynthia Brandon walked out of that apartment Monday past. Today is Thursday. On Tuesday, one of my men, Detective Gonzalez, saw Cynthia Brandon walking in Central Park with a man. If you remember, Tuesday was a lousy March day with snow—not so different from today, but they were holding hands. Everything lovey-dovey, except that Gonzalez thought he recognized the man. The man rang a bell somewhere. Anyway, Gonzalez has a fantastic memory for faces and he came back here and went through some of the books. He found this in the Interpol book, an album of mug shots that we get from Interpol twice a year."

Rothschild opened his desk drawer, took out a folder and from it a glossy photograph, which he handed to me. It was a picture of a good-looking dark man, with strong features and a pleasant smile—the kind of a face I have always liked and that I always compare favorably with my own.

"Does it do anything to you?" Rothschild asked.

"It makes me envious. That's the way I would have looked if I had picked the right parents. Who is he?"

"His real name is Valento Corsica, and he was born in Ragusa. That's a town in Sicily. He was educated there, Milan and London. Perfect English, French—and, of course, Italian. Polished, well-mannered, and usually goes under the name of Count Gambion de Fonti. A count, yet. No criminal record, but three arrests by Italian police, two by Scotland Yard and one by the Sureté. Nothing ever held, but Interpol wired us over three thousand words on him."

"What's his line," I asked, "the rich heiress gambit?"

"Oh, no—not at all, Harvey. Not one bit. In fact, in a poker game, Valento could cover all of E.C. Brandon's bets and a good bit more. As for his profession—leadership."

[44]

"Leadership?"

"Leadership." Rothschild managed a smile. Not much of a smile, but for Rothschild it was a real achievement. "You see, Harvey, according to Interpol, for the past fifteen years or so, Valento Corsica has been trained to take over the leadership of the Mafia. Schooled, trained, groomed—"

"Mafia? You're putting me on."

"Mafia. Syndicate. Call it what you wish, Harvey—Valento Corsica was groomed to lead it. Twelve weeks ago, Joe Asianti, the incumbent, had a stroke and went to his Maker. Last Tuesday, Detective Frank Gonzalez sees the heir apparent walking in the park with Cynthia Brandon and thank God he has a good enough memory for faces to spot both of them. So, you see, Harvey, either you come clean with me, or so help me God, I'll call in a cop to slug you and then charge you with assaulting an officer with a deadly weapon and then throw you into one of our own little detention cells, right here at the nineteenth, where you could sit for a week before anyone knew you were here."

"You wouldn't do that."

"Want to try, Harvey?"

"You'd call in a cop to slug me? I don't believe it."

"That's right Harvey. So believe it."

"OK."

"OK what?"

"I'll talk. I'm no good for a holdout. One twist of the arm and I break. E.C. Brandon thinks his daughter's been kidnapped. I'm sworn not to tell the cops—so now you can see how deceitful I am."

"What?"

"That's him. I don't think she's been kidnapped."

"What do you mean, that's him?"

[45]

"I mean it's Brandon's notion that she's been kidnapped. If I thought for one moment that she really has been kidnapped, you'd have to work me over with your rubber hoses to get it out of me. But I don't think so, and your report from Gonzalez doesn't sound like any kidnapped girl."

"No, it doesn't. And furthermore, we don't use rubber hoses. But there's one little hole in your story, Harvey."

"I know."

"You," Rothschild agreed. "How do you come into it? No stolen property—no jewels to be fenced. How do you come into it?"

"I know. Brandon carries kidnap insurance."

"What?"

I nodded, and I told him the whole silly story, and he just sat there behind his old, beat-up desk, nursing what was left of his glass of milk, and regarding me with sour disbelief. When I had finished, he took a deep breath, got up and left the room, and returned a moment late with a carton of milk, from which he poured a fresh glass.

"All right, what did you leave out, Harvey?"

I had left out the hundred thousand dollars, and I intended it to remain left out.

"That's the story."

"So that's the story. Just where do you think you go from here?"

"I don't know."

"Maybe you forgot. Try to remember, Harvey."

"The trouble is that you have me pegged for being smart. I get one or two breaks, and the word is around that I solve problems."

"Not smart—crafty, Harvey. I don't trust you. But that's my cop nature. I don't trust anyone."

[46]

"Lieutenant," I said very sincerely, "I don't have one blessed notion where that girl is, and the fact that she is holding hands in Central Park with the new top man in the Syndicate is news to me. Scout's honor."

Rothschild did not deign to reply. He simply looked at me, something at which he is very good indeed.

Chapter 4

Friday I checked records, read about the Brandon family and skimmed through three books on the Syndicate; and then I called Dr. Fred Bronstein, the psychoanalyst on East 75th Street.

"I can't talk to you now, Harvey. I am with a patient."

I called him a halfhour later.

"Harvey," he said petulantly, "you know that during my professional day I welcome only professional calls."

"Well, how do you know that this isn't a professional call?"

"Look, Harvey, I don't have time to horse around."

"I'm not horsing around. I'm in trouble. I want to see you."

"It's got to cost you thirty dollars."

"Oh, no."

"Oh, yes," he said.

"It used to be twenty."

"Well, a quart of milk used to be twelve cents, Harvey."

"Not in my time."

"Thirty, Harvey. Take it or leave it."

[49]

I took it, and he complained that he would be giving me part of his Saturday morning.

"You don't know how I fight to keep Saturday morning for squash," he said. And the following morning I was ready to believe him; the rackets were there and he had his tennis shoes on. "I could squeeze five sessions out of a Saturday morning, Harvey," he assured me. "That would amount to one hundred and fifty dollars—but money isn't everything."

"No?"

"No, Harvey. Absolutely not. To you money is a symbol. Some people would call you chintzy—but that's not a very acute diagnosis. It's your attitude toward money, the attitude in itself—"

"Whose time are we one?"

"Yours, Harvey."

"Well, why don't you let me talk? And it's not money. The fact is that people don't like me. You take this Lieutenant Rothschild—you know, he terrifies me—"

"Why don't you lie down, Harvey."

"Thanks," I said, and I stretched out on his couch. "He's got ulcers, and he looks at me and right away I can see that he's blaming me for the goddamn ulcers—"

"The same Lieutenant Rothschild, Harvey?"

"The same one. My God, you don't think there are two of them, do you?"

"I don't think it's profitable to discuss Lieutenant Rothschild, Harvey. We've been through all that in the past. It's yourself that we're interested in—"

"It's myself that I am talking about. It's what myself does to people like Rothschild."

"Harvey, I told you—"

"All right. All right. Rothschild—"

"Harvey, I am going to play squash," he said, grabbing his racket. "It is no bloody damn use. I try to make an hour productive and you spend it hating this Rothschild. I am going to play—"

"On my money?"

"It's free. It's a gift. Now, out with you!"

I walked all the distance to the Donnell Library and took Lucille Dempsey to lunch at the Oak Room of the St. Regis. She accompanied me in a rather dazed state, and after she had looked at the menu, asked me whether I was all right.

"Of course I am."

"Harvey, this lunch can cost you fifteen dollars."

"I know," I answered moodily. "I know that. Go ahead. Eat. Enjoy it."

"How can I enjoy it? Every bite will cut you like a twinge of pain."

"OK—OK. What's the difference? Do you know where this Cynthia Brandon kid is? She's walking around in Central Park with the new king of the Mafia."

She looked at me with motherly concern, and I told her the rest of it. Then she ordered lunch. Then we ate and she turned the matter over in her mind. Like most superior women, she is always inventing childish ways to make me feel smarter than she is.

"Harvey, where did Cynthia go to college?" she asked me.

"Ann Bromley, which is a small college up in Connecticut, near Danbury. Four, five hundred students, all girls, all very rich."

"She graduated?"

"Nope. She parted. They didn't dare to throw her out, with the Brandon money behind her and she didn't want to stay."

"Why did they want to throw her out?"

"Because she tried to integrate the place. She turned up for her junior year with five Negro girls, wrote her own check for their tuition, and demanded that they be enrolled as students. The whole damn school nearly got a stroke. She threatened to blow the lid off with newspaper stories, and then the old man was called into the act and he beat her down."

"Oh? You know, Harvey, I am beginning to like your Cynthia. Was there a lot of wild talk about her using pot?"

"How did you know?"

"A kid like that has to try it. Do you have pictures of her, Harvey?"

I took out the pictures and showed them to her.

"I have a notion," Lucille said, "so tomorrow morning, at ten o'clock, Harvey, we are going bicycling in Central Park. You do ride a bike?"

"Of course I ride a bike. And what do we find—Cynthia holding hands with Valento Corsica?"

"Maybe we just have a date, Harvey. It is Sunday, and you can afford to take a Sunday off, can't you?"

So instead of sleeping through Sunday morning, as any civilized human being has the right to do, I was finishing breakfast at the zoo with Lucille Dempsey, who is not by any means one of these tiny, skinny kids, but a solid five-foot-seven, one hundred and thirty pounds—and who, by virtue of this, had a bowl of oatmeal, two eggs, four strips of bacon, two slices of toast and two cups of coffee. As well as a large orange juice for a starter. All of which I watched from above my single cup of black coffee with a mixture of horror and envy.

"You would feel better, Harvey," she said, "if you had a

[52]

good breakfast. Breakfast is the most important meal of the day."

"Of which my mother never failed to remind me."

"Well, your mother was right."

"No one ever told you that the worst way in the world to get a man is to remind him that his mother was right?"

"I am not at all sure that I want to get you, Harvey. The fact that I feel a certain tenderness toward you does not necessarily mean that I wish to marry you. Do you have the pictures of Cynthia with you?"

"Why?"

"I want one."

"Now?"

"Now. You know, you always ask the obvious, Harvey."

I gave her the picture of Cynthia, which she slipped into her purse, and finally she finished the interminable breakfast and we began to walk to the boathouse, where the bike livery kept itself. The weather had changed, and this was a crisp, cool sunny morning, and since the Mayor kept the cars out of the park, the air was clean as crystal. Lucille wore a plaid skirt and a white turtleneck sweater and she was a pleasure to look at if you didn't know her character, and had a surprising figure for a girl who ate three solid meals a day the way she did. Even the fact that she wore flat-heeled shoes and walked with a long, athletic stride did not make her less of a beautiful woman; and I decided that it was a simple fact of perfection that depressed me.

"Why," I asked her, "do you need the photograph? Do you suppose she's still drifting around the park with Count Gambion de Fonti, alias Valento Corsica?"

"Now, Harvey, just be patient."

"And why the bikes?"

"Because it's fun, Harvey. Bikes are fun. There is very little left that is really fun. Bikes are fun. There is also a Be-in. The bikes will take us to the Be-in."

"What is a Be-in?"

"All in good time, Harvey. All in good time."

Behind the boathouse, we joined the crowd of the young, the old and the middle-aged, who were queued up to rent bikes. It was no atmosphere in which to remain depressed, and I realized that the simple fact of one's presence in the park on a Sunday morning evoked gaiety. They brought us two beautiful British bikes with handbrakes, and a few minutes later, we were peddling north on the East Drive.

"Once around," Lucille said, "and then we'll cut into the Sheep Meadow from the west."

"And then?"

"And then we're a part of the Be-in."

"And what in hell is a Be-in?"

"It's something you do when your heart is filled with love instead of hate, and anyway, Harvey, you are too old and cynical for me to explain it to you, so why don't we wait."

We had reached the top of the hill behind the Museum now, and we shifted into high gear and raced north. This was not something I had ever done before, not as an adult in Central Park with the park all to myself and not an auto in sight, and I saluted the mayor and tried to catch Lucille. She was in better shape than I was—I suppose because her thoughts were purer and because of all the damned vegetables she ate, and as we approached 110th Street, I begged her to take it easier.

"How are we going to see Cynthia at fifty miles an hour?"

"Harvey!"

"We'll walk up this hill—just to keep in practice. When

[54]

Sunday's over, I have to walk again. For a whole week I'll be walking."

But by the time we had rounded the northern end of the park and were on our way back downtown on the West Drive, I had got my second wind, and I realized that I felt better and more relaxed than in a long, long time. We coasted down the long hill to 72nd Street, up a part of the way toward the Sheep Meadow, and then we walked, leading the bikes. There was a general convergence toward the Sheep Meadow, youngsters for the most part, some on bikes but most of them on foot, boys and girls holding hands, most of them relaxed and smiling and at peace with themselves and the world.

Some of the boys were bearded; some of the girls wore long, flowing kimono-type things; they were all a little beat and dressed beat to one extent or another, and they had flowers in their buttonholes, pinned on to their clothes, twined in their hair, and very often painted onto their cheeks. They drifted toward the knoll at the southeast edge of the Sheep Meadow, where well over a thousand of them had already gathered.

"This is a Be-in?" I asked Lucille.

"That's right."

On the knoll, they had instruments, mostly drums, and they kept up a steady beat. A sort of sound came out of it. "Ba-na-na," as near as I could make out, over and over again. Some of the kids had signs. One sign said LOVE, DON'T HATE. Another sign said, LOVE IS ALL.

As we pushed our bikes toward the knoll, I asked one of the kids, "What is it?"

"Be-in."

"He says it's a Be-in," I told Lucille.

"I told you so."

"What's a Be-in?" I asked him.

"Too old, Dad."

"What?"

"You, Dad."

"Too old to understand," the girl with him said.

"I told you," said Lucille.

Another kid, helpfully, said, "Be-in is love, Dad."

"Oh, don't complicate it, feel it," a tall, handsome girl said.

"Feel it, Dad. This is a good place."

It became a crowded place now, approaching the knoll. There were twenty or thirty cops spaced around but nothing for them to do. No one was doing anything in particular except that the little group on the top of the knoll beat the drums.

"I'm looking for my friend," Lucille said.

"This place is full of friends," a bearded, redheaded boy who looked like a Viking in blue jeans, assured her. "Full of friends, Sister. Just feel it."

"They call you Sister and me Dad," I complained.

"You're old, Dad," a girl said. She had two long yellow braids, the face of an angel, and a pink muumuu. There was a silver spot pasted to the center of her forehead. "It's not the years," she added.

"My friend's name is Cynthia," Lucille said.

"Cynthia what?"

"Brandon."

"I'll keep it in mind," the Viking grinned.

We walked our bikes through the crowd, and it was certainly the best-natured crowd I had ever seen. Bikers like ourselves, older folk on foot, kids of every description, moth-

[56]

ers with carriages—all drifted into the crowd. The engaging good humor and good nature of the insiders was irresistible, and no one was angry or petulant—though by now there were three or four thousand people around the knoll. Lucille stuck to the bedecked hippies, and asked her question endlessly and patiently.

"Seen Cynthia anywhere?"

"Sorry, sweetheart."

"Ba-na-na!" they chanted. "Ba-na-na!"

It was late enough now for the staid and well-groomed strollers from Fifth Avenue to reach the scene, and they watched with dignified disapproval, asking the cops for explanations. But the cops shrugged it off. "As long as they keep the peace," a cop said, "they can dress the way they want to."

"Cynthia?" Lucille asked for the fortieth time.

"Are you going to keep that up all morning?" I demanded, a little irritated. "What do you expect to happen?"

"I expect someone to know Cynthia."

"Why?"

"That's why they call you Dad," Lucille said. "It's not the way you look. Mostly, you don't even look grown up—"

"What!"

"Come on—you know what I mean. You're very nice-looking, Harvey, and you even look a little bit like that actor —what's his name?—George Gizzard."

"Grizzard, you mean, George Grizzard."

"Well, it's something like that, isn't it? And you do resemble him—"

Well, it's very hard to get angry with a girl who tells you that you resemble a good-looking actor, because the truth of it is that no one looks like an actor except another actor.

[57]

"—but you feel old, Harvey." She buttonholed a boy tall enough to be a basketball player, and he had an artificial daisy in each ear. "Where's Cynthia?"

"Cynthia? Man, this is a big meadow."

"Well, where is she?" Lucille insisted.

"Well, you know—she doesn't have a station. She could be anywhere. It's a free country."

"Have you seen her?" Lucille insisted.

"Hey, Dolly," he called out to a light brown Negro girl, who wore a crown of woven pink carnations, "where's Cynthia?"

The girl with the carnations waved a languid hand. "Beautiful," she said, "it's all beautiful with elements and beingness."

"Cynthia," I reminded her.

"Isn't she here?"

"Look, Dad," said the basketball player, pointing to a couple with their arms entwined, swaying to the beat of the music, "that's Don Cooper. He and his girl are writing a show—way out, off Broadway, cuts like a knife—cuts right in where the decay is and out it comes. Cynthia promised to back it for him when it's ready. So you want to know where Cynthia is—ask them."

"Thanks, chum," Lucille said. "I'll say a prayer for you to score high. Fifty shots in the next game."

"Bless you, bubby," he grinned.

"Well?" she said to me as we walked toward the songwriter.

"There you are," I nodded, "You wouldn't want me to marry anyone as smart as you. I'd be out of it from the word go."

"Just so long as you know, Harvey."

[58]

"I know."

The songwriter had a yellow beard. His girl had the word *love* spelled out in lipstick on each cheek. They were both about nineteen. When Lucille asked them about Cynthia, they studied her very carefully and then they studied me, and then the kid said, "What's Dad here?" nodding at me.

"What do you mean, what am I?"

"You fuzz?"

The girl said, "He's the new look if he is. He's a doll. Come over here, Doll." It was the first word of encouragement I had received since I set foot on the damned meadow, so I wheeled my bike over to her. She took out her lipstick and painted a five-petaled flower on my forehead. We gathered a small crowd at first and then they drifted off. She painted the word love on one cheek.

"Harvey, you're sweet," Lucille said.

"He's not fuzz," the boy said.

"How do you know?" I asked him.

"He's an insurance investigator," Lucille said. "Show him your credentials, Harvey." I showed my credentials.

"What about Cynthia?"

"Well," I said, "she walked out of her apartment on Monday. Here it is Sunday. No one had heard a word from her since."

"Do you blame her?"

"I don't blame her. But suppose she's in trouble. Who's going to back your show?"

"What makes you think she's in trouble?" the girl asked.

"Look, Dad," the boy began, but the girl stopped him and said with some asperity, "He's absolutely right. Who else is going to back your show? If you're an insurance investigator, where's your beef about Cynthia?"

"She's insured."

"That's a cold-blooded attitude, if I may say so."

"Why?" Lucille demanded. "At least we're trying to find her and help her if she's in trouble."

"She's right," Don admitted.

"You got any idea where she might be?" I asked.

"No one has. We've been trying to reach her all week. We decided that if there was any place she'd be, it would be out here at the Be-in."

"She's not here," the girl said.

"We've been watching all day."

"Asking."

"I mean searching for her."

"Goddamn it," the boy said, "she's disappeared."

"Fled," the girl said. "You ever met her father and mother? Fled. Fled."

"What was she hung up on?" I asked them.

Beardsley, Charlie Brown, *The Village Voice*—"

"Civil rights," the girl said.

"Hermann Hesse."

"English music hall songs."

"You really think she's in trouble?" the boy asked.

"Computer dating," the girl said.

Chapter 5

I half-expected that at ten o'clock on a Monday morning, I would find her sober if hung over; but such was not my good fortune. How many Alice Brandon had had, I can't say. As she was drinking vodka, the odor was not overwhelming, but her center of gravity swayed pleasantly, and she said slowly and precisely, "Dear Mr. Krim—how very good of you to return! You are enchanted with me. Wouldn't that be a laugh? Do you know, after you left I decided that you looked more like Lawrence Harvey, only he is better looking, you know, and I think it's only because you have the same name—"

"Harvey Krim, Mrs. Brandon."

"Naturally." She was wearing a crepe at-home rig in a combination of lavender, violet and magenta, and she insisted that I have breakfast with her.

"I had breakfast. Coffee will be fine."

"Orange juice—half-vodka? Dear Mr. Krim, please don't allow me to drink alone at this hour of the morning."

The breakfast room was a glassed-in, heated terrace, with

bridges and roofs for scenery, Italian tile on the floor, and a breakfast table of cast aluminum and thick glass. A mixture of white and hybrid lavender roses were the order of the day, and I told myself that with a minimum of effort, I could fall into the habits of the rich. I wondered aloud why Mrs. Brandon did not enjoy it more.

"Because my husband's a louse, Harvey boy. Any more questions?"

The butler, Jonas, was serving coffee and eggs and sausages and bacon—the last three items I declined and she was drinking her nourishment—and the comments on his boss's character appeared not to disturb him at all.

"A few."

"Then hold them until this creep gets out of here. I mean Jonas Biddle, butler. I can't stand butlers, least of all this one. He's Brandon's intelligence service, only he's stupid." She turned to the butler and told him flatly, "Oh, get to hell out of here, will you, Jonas."

His face set, he marched out.

"Why does he take it?" I asked her.

"He's paid to take it, Harvey. I would adore for him to quit—but he takes it. You're not touching your orange juice."

"At this hour of the morning it would destroy me."

"Poor boy—I'll use it." She picked it up and took a healthy drink. "Ask, Harvey."

"Computer dating."

"What the devil is that? Oh—you mean that compatibility thing with the computers. Cynthia was very big on that."

"Why?"

"I suppose she figured she could meet someone who did not know she was E.C.'s daughter. The same way she gave herself the nickname 'Jake.' She told everyone at Ann Brom-

[62]

ley College that Jake was her name. It was the one name E.C. thoroughly hated."

"But why the computer? Certainly she met enough boys."

"Harvey—have you ever explored the male market today? It is not to make a girl explode with joy. E.C. has a summer place at Green Farms—"

"Where's that?"

"The east end of Westport, Connecticut. Actually, it's in trust for Cynthia from her mother, and it's more like a jail than a place of joy. So tell me where Cynthia meets sympatico boys? Just tell me?"

"Her father's friends?"

"Some day you must meet her daddy's friends and their offspring."

"Your friends?"

"I drink my friends, Daddy-o. Ah, come on, Harvey, have one orange juice."

When I got downstairs, Sergeant Kelly was waiting for me in his neo-police Brooks Brothers tweeds, and he said, "Well, what have you got to say now, Krim."

"You know," I told him, "when they set up a police state here, Rothschild and you will be president and vice-president."

"That's great. The Lieutenant always wanted to be president. Only don't think we are playing for marbles, Harvey boy. Four well known torpedoes have joined the tourists who feel that this is Fun City. They are all Texas kids: Jack Selby, who calls himself Ringo, Freddy Upson, otherwise known as the Ghost, Billy the Kid, who has the reputation of having performed twenty-seven contracts, and Joey Earp, who calls himself the Descendent, maybe because he watches TV between executions."

[63]

"All right. So you are being invaded. Is that any reason to give me the business out here on the sidewalk?"

"No one is giving you the business, Harvey. You know, you are paranoid about cops."

"Who isn't?"

"I'm not. Now listen—these are four boys from Texas and none of them are Syndicate. They're a part of the Fats Coventry mob, which is very big down there and bases itself in Houston. The Syndicate wants in there, and Fats has been too tough for them."

"I also remember the Alamo."

"Don't be a wise guy, Harvey."

"Well, what the hell shall I be? Why don't you and Rothschild get off my back and stop with the *True Detective* stories. I got my work to do."

"That's just it, Harvey. Your work. Where Valento Corsica is—that's where we think your Cynthia Brandon is, and that is where these four hoodlums are headed and there is something very big coming up, and the Lieutenant thinks you are smart—"

"Tell the Lieutenant I am stupid," I said, trying to make it sound like a snarl. Kelly grinned. I turned my back on him and walked away.

When I got to my office, it was 11:30 A.M., and Lucille was waiting for me. Mazie Gilman, outside, said it was my sister.

"Do you have a sister, Harvey?" Lucille asked me. "I really know so little about you."

"Sister!" I said. "You know, it's the way that YMCA mind of yours works. You couldn't just say you were a friend. Did the library fire you?"

"No, the library did not fire me. And it would be YWCA, and a sense of propriety—something you would hardly understand—made me say I was your sister."

[64]

"And here you are."

"And here I am, Harvey Krim, because I have eleven days of sick leave coming to me and a perfect attendance record, and do you know what I thought of just when I was falling asleep—and I would have called you right then and there, but I thought perhaps mercifully you had gone to sleep at a reasonable hour—"

"Yes," I interrupted.

"Yes, what?"

"Yes, I know what you thought about when you were falling asleep and do you realize that if everyone talked like you the structure of the English language would disappear."

"I don't think that's very kind."

"Well—all right. You thought about computer dating."

She dropped into a chair across the desk from me and faced me earnestly. "Harvey," she said, "do you know this is a very fascinating job you have. Of course you thought of computer dating. We both thought about it. But why?"

"Because as much as you might like a super highway, you make out with a little dirt road when there's nothing better."

"Oh, Harvey," she grinned. "You do clutch at fancy metaphors, don't you. Of course, you're wrong. If one must travel the big highway, one finds it."

"One does."

"Oh, yes, Harvey. It's not at all as complicated as you make it out to be. It's just a question of point of view. From one point of view nothing at all makes sense. E.C. Brandon's daughter disappears. She is seen in Central Park holding hands with that Count—what did you say his name was?"

"Valento Corsica, alias Count Gambion de Fonti."

"Yes, Mr. Corsica, who is the heir to the Syndicate—or Mafia. Which is it?"

"You take your choice."

"Then she doesn't show up at the Be-in. Do you know, Harvey, if I were Cynthia, I would let nothing short of disaster keep me away from the Be-in. Don't you see—a Be-in complements someone like Cynthia, wholly, perfectly."

"Why?"

"Oh, because everyone needs love, Harvey, and Cynthia needs it so desperately."

"Everyone?" I asked her.

"Of course everyone. Now just listen to me for a moment, Harvey." She was more excited than I had ever known her to be. Her face was flushed, and her honey-colored hair, loosely tied behind her neck, glowed in the shaft of sunlight that came through the one window with which my office was blessed. She was so painlessly, unconsciously beautiful that I almost interrupted her again, this time to ask her to marry me. Fortunately, I regained my senses.

"Before I came here, I stopped off at the Library, Harvey—"

"You said you were on sick leave."

"Of course. I let everyone know I had a dreadful headache and was only stopping by for a moment."

"Perfidy!" I exclaimed. "From Lucille Dempsey, white, Presbyterian New England American—"

"Oh, Harvey, that was a white lie. Really, you are the most difficult person to understand or talk to."

"I am?"

"Do listen to me now. I stopped by at the Library, where we have a social studies room, and there we keep a file of computer oddities and social influences. I Xeroxed the three major dating service applications, and here they are. Two of them are for age eighteen to thirty, and the third is for age eighteen to twenty-seven. Most people are quite conservative

[66]

and are inclined to take these things as a joke, but I have learned that they are a very thriving business. Their purpose is very direct and simple—to bring together men and women who have various tastes and desires and status yearnings in common."

"I know all that," I protested, "and it doesn't take us one step closer to the question of where Cynthia is."

"Doesn't it? Well, look, Harvey, everyone thinks they know all about this computer dating. But sitting here for the past hour and waiting for you, I have been going through these questionnaires. Don't just brush them off. They are quite extraordinary. They not only allow for similarities, they also point up dissimilarities—so that people can come together as complementary factors. And that's not as crazy as it sounds. Just think of the attraction you have for me—"

"I am thinking about it," I said.

"So they analyze compatibility on the basis of difference as well as similarity. Take for instance, analysis of character. This one forces you to analyze yourself—so that you can project the image of yourself as you see yourself—"

"I always thought the gift was to see ourselves as others see us."

"Very true, Harvey, but here the point is not to reveal the utter truth but to match A with B. Do you understand—to match?"

I stared at her very thoughtfully and nodded. "Go on," I said.

"All right. Now here we have nineteen words, as follows: *athletic, restless, studious, taciturn, reckless, stubborn, optimistic, nervous, lonely, ambitious, sociable, reserved, generous, egotistical, moody, meticulous, visionary,* and *affectionate.* You are asked to choose the six that best describe you.

Now I suppose the justifying psychological base is that one will choose less of himself than what he desires from a mate—"

"Which doesn't mean a marriage that will work."

"Of course not, Harvey—I don't think anyone knows what on earth all this means, and as far as I am concerned it's a gimmick. Absolutely a gimmick. But right now, I am trying to be helpful—"

"Go on, Girl Detective."

"Well, take this status business. The questionnaires try to place the people in status slots. They ask if you have a credit card. They list various cars—*Continental, Cadillac, Plymouth, Ford, Chevvy, Rambler, XK-E, Volkswagen, Triumph, Mustang—which is your choice?*"

"I wonder what Cynthia would make of that—"

"Or Valento Corsica. Now suppose you begin the week with two hundred dollars in your pocket. How much of it are you likely to spend on the following: *dates, tips, books, records, movies, car rentals, live theater, cosmetics, travel, cabs?*"

"Interests? Hobbies?" I asked.

"All of it here. Most of the tests ask you to rate yourself by declaring an order of preference. Consider the following interests—*medicine, law, music, literature, accounting, golf, history, current events, war now, past war, drama, skiing, skating, ice, wheels, teaching, bridge, poker, canasta, French, Italian, German, Greek, swimming*—and so forth and so on. Which is number one and which is number two and which is number three—do I make any sense at all, Harvey?"

"More and more. How do they get a sort of emotional compatability, or doesn't that interest them?"

"That's not reversible, Harvey. That's direct. They all ask

race—*Caucasian, Negro, Oriental.* But one of them does reverse it. *What do you prefer?* They list all the major religions and ask you to choose one, but then two of them supply a second identical listing for you to choose your date's religion. They have four categories of height and again, most of them have an identical list for preference. Also with age—two lists. By the way, just how rich would this Valento Corsica be?"

"You name it."

"Richer than E.C. Brandon?"

"It's not a question of having, Lucille," I explained. "It's a question of control, who controls more money. He does—Brother Corsica."

"Here we are—*What is your attitude toward money? I want to be very rich. I want to be moderately rich. I don't care whether I am ever rich. I disdain wealth*—that in one two of the tests. And conversely, *I come from a very rich family, upper middle class, middle class, laboring class.* One of the tests goes into the father's profession: not categories but open spaces. You fill in, but for the date, a series of categories to choose from. Harvey, it's clearer and clearer."

"Or muddier and muddier. Doesn't anything fix it to the American scene?"

"You would think so, wouldn't you, Harvey? But only if you want to accept the cliché about baseball and apple pie. In the category of cultural background, they ask: *If you have a choice, which will you attend—Shakespeare live, ballet, a baseball game, a prize fight, a symphony?* Give that one to an American college graduate, a citizen of Ghana and a Finn, and nationality won't mean one blessed thing, Harvey."

"But suppose it was their ploy—"

"Do you know why, Harvey? You do see why, don't you?"

"All right—just leave their reasons alone for the moment.

[69]

Just suppose they do it—why answer truthfully? Why not fake it out from the word go?"

"Because they're smart, Harvey. They wanted it of a piece. These things have to have a pattern—"

"Of course!" I exclaimed. "The computer is programmed. That's what we keep forgetting, that these damn machines can't think. They can only give out what is put in, and in this case they are programmed for a series of patterns. Corsica's advisors can't guess the particular pattern, so he's honest. He answers the questions truthfully. What about drinking—that's international enough?"

"They all have a category for drinking. *Excessively, more than usual, moderate, infrequently, or not at all.* Also attitudes: *Do you approve of drinking? Whisky? Brandy? Wine?* Not all of them have that but two of them do. Also gambling —*not at all, moderately, excessively.* Does your Cynthia gamble?"

"No mention of it. Why should she? That's not considered kicks in her crowd."

"Does Corsica?"

I thought about that for a while. Of course he would not gamble. Owning half the State of Nevada, he would be an idiot to gamble. I said to Lucille, "Are you trying to tell me that E.C. Brandon and the Mafia would produce the same type offspring?"

"Of course not, Harvey. But that doesn't mean that they would not fill out these questionnaires in the same way."

"That is reaching."

"Well, isn't the whole point of this to reach?"

"OK—where do we start?"

"With the biggest, Harvey," she said eagerly. "Computer Social Studies—in forty-seven states, Mexico and Canada. Address is 599 Fifth Avenue."

[70]

"That's the Scribner Building. That's an odd place for it—one of the very old, Victorian places left on Fifth Avenue."

"They want respectibility, Harvey, naturally. And you will buy me lunch."

We went to the Woman's Exchange, and then we walked down Fifth Avenue to the Scribner Building. But Computer Social Studies was a disappointment. In a tiny office, no more than ten by twelve feet, an old lady peered at us nearsightedly from a small cave in a pile of baled questionnaires and old files. Not a computer in sight.

"Three of you?" she asked.

"Two of us," Lucille answered sweetly, "Mr. Krim and myself."

"Are you cops?" the old lady asked, polishing her thick lenses. "Dear me, my eyes are not what they were. If you are cops, Stanley says you got nothing on us because what we are doing is absolutely one hundred percent legal—did I hear the door close?" she asked Lucille.

"No, ma'am," I replied.

"Where is the other one?"

"Only the two of us."

"Three of you came in."

"No—really," Lucille said. "Two of us. Only two of us."

"Who is Stanley?"

"He's my son, of course." The desk was covered with papers, and she went through them hopelessly. "You know, it's Stanley's desk. He's disorderly."

"Where is Stanley?" I asked her.

"He was always disorderly. He was a disorderly child. Do you know, he would do his homework and put it away, and then he would simply forget where it was at. 'Stanley,' I said to him, 'do your homework and give it to me.' Well, do you know—"

[71]

"Where is Stanley?" I begged her.

"Oh? Stanley?"

"We want to know where your son is, Mrs.—" Lucille said gently.

"I'm Ellie."

"Well, it would be nicer if we knew your last name," Lucille said "I mean, you are entitled to that."

"You're a nice girl," the old lady said. "I wish that Stanley had met you before he became engaged. That's where he is now."

"Being engaged?"

"Oh, no. No. He became engaged last month. Now he's out in Brooklyn at Mr. Bumper's place, where Mr. Bumper has this IBM machine. Stanley has an idea that he can program this machine to do the dating surveys, and you see his secretary became pregnant, so I am here for a while, but you know it's really a different kind of a machine. Stanley is very bright, but—"

"My dear lady," I interrupted, "here on your test paper, it says, *Computer Social Studies—in Forty-seven states, Mexico and Canada.*"

She smiled brightly. "That was Stanley's idea. Don't you think it's very clever?"

"Why not fifty states?" Lucille asked.

"Stanley thought forty-seven would be psychologically more effective. Don't you agree?"

We agreed and we left. We walked uptown to Compudate, Inc. at 57th Street and Madison Avenue, which was a small but going concern. They even had a computer. A fat, smiling man called Mr. Ready was the manager. Three other people worked in the office, and our hopes rose slightly.

Mr. Ready gave us his card. "Ready on the right, Ready on the left," he said. Then he smiled. He smiled with his whole face. We mentioned that we had just come from Computer Social Studies, and he smiled understandingly. "That outfit gives the whole industry a bad name," he smiled, "but when you launch your craft on the wave of the future, you get every element. Think of it—for the first time in human history, we have an opportunity to reduce the random factor in mating to absolute zero. Of course, the experiment is still in its infancy. We have worlds to conquer. Think of it—an opportunity to marry a girl you've never seen before, yet with the total, unshakable certainty that she shares your every thought, likes the same food, shares your appetite for sex, wants the same—why do you shudder, Mrs.—?" he asked Lucille, smiling warmly.

"Miss Dempsey."

"Miss Dempsey. Shall we fear the future? Or should we rather walk forward with firm steps to welcome it and embrace it."

"That's a wonderful thought," Lucille agreed.

"Do you represent a school? Or perhaps you have a territorial interest? This is the time to get in, now, at the beginning—as if you were standing beside Marconi or Thomas Edison—"

"I'm an insurance investigator," I told him. "My name is Harvey Krim."

His face froze but the smile remained. It now became a frozen smile, and it was a remarkable thing to see. Still smiling, he asked coldly, "What can I do for you, sir?"

"Believe me, you have done nothing wrong," I hastened to assure him. "We are interested in the loss of a rather expensive fur coat, and there is some reason to believe that the girl who reported its loss used your dating service. That's all. If we could simply find the man's name—"

"Why don't you ask her?"

"Oh, we did. First thing. But I think the name was part of it—at least, we can find no address. Here are my credentials."

He examined them thoughtfully. The card the company gives me folds in two, and I always keep a ten-dollar bill in the fold. When he returned it to me, his frozen smile had relaxed into a beam and the ten-dollar bill was missing.

"All right—who's the girl?" His smile was now a smile of complicity, and I wondered whether he ever accepted anyone or anything at its face value.

"Cynthia Brandon."

"Ah-hah!" The receptionist, the girl closest to us, who doubled as a typist and an answering service, was listening so intently that her ears practically quivered. Ready said to her, "Turn it off, Nosey. You'll strain your eardrums." And to us, "Come into my office where the third balcony is not crowded." His humor was as heavy as he was, and from the corner of my eye, I saw the receptionist stick her tongue out after him.

His office was tasteless in chrome and glass. "I like the look of tomorrow," he said, waving an arm. "Sit down, sit down. You struck paydirt. Cynthia Brandon—what kind of coat?"

"Russian sable—worth seventy-two thousand dollars," Lucille said without blinking an eyelash. Her Presbyterian ethic was crumbling visibly.

"That's the way it goes. It takes talent to spend money like that. How much did you say?"

"Seventy-two thousand."

"Ready on the right, Ready on the left," he quipped—his sense of humor never failing him. "You know why I remember that one?"

We both waited.

[74]

"Because they matched and married. Or at least that was on the schedule."

"You're telling me Cynthia Brandon is married?" I demanded.

"Scheduled, scheduled, brother Krim. You don't find me giving false information to a shamus. That's what you are, isn't it?" he asked uncertainly.

"On the West Coast. Here I'm an insurance investigator. Who is this *they?*"

"They?"

"You just said they matched. Cynthia Brandon and who?"

"That would be in the matched files." He smiled reassuringly. "When I said you struck paydirt, I meant just that—paydirt. Never worry about our files." He switched on his intercom and said to one of the girls outside, "Sylvia, bring me Cynthia Brandon's file and its match."

A moment or two later, she entered with two file folders, which she dropped onto his desk. I reached, but he covered them with two fat paws, shook his head and smiled. "Oh, no. Confidence. No eyes but ours rest on the files. Ask me questions—I will answer them so long as no sacred confidence is violated."

"That's very noble of you," Lucille said.

"We try, we try," he said. "Praise us not with too much honey lest the bees come with their foul stings—Dickens."

"It's very unusual to quote Dickens," Lucille said.

"Oh, yes. Thank you. Here we are." He opened one of the files. "Cynthia Brandon. I select at random—Section three, Category six, Question: *What do you regard as the major source of your frustration?* Answer: *The Establishment.* Now I turn to the companion folder. Section three, Category six. Answer: *The Establishment.*"

[75]

"And whose folder is that?" Lucille asked.

"Remarkable young man. His name is Gambion de Fonti. Italian, but very old, respectable family. Barrels of money. That's our service—money goes to money, order, sanity."

"Gambion de Fonti," I said.

"Gambion de Fonti. Section two, Question: *Do you want money?* Answer: *No, I have all I need.* The other folder, Section two—"

"I am sure we understand," Lucille said politely. "Cynthia Brandon has all the money she needs. So does Gambion de Fonti. By the way, Mr. Ready, did you know he was a count?"

"No. You don't say so."

"I do indeed."

"Then you know him?"

"Let's say we know of him," I said. "Of course you have his address?"

"Of course—right here. The Ritzhampton, at Sixty-fourth and Madison."

"It would be the Ritzhampton," Lucille nodded. "Where else does one stay?"

Mr. Ready's mind was racing. "Do you know," he said, "a combination of Cynthia Brandon and a real, legitimate count could put this company on the map. But I mean on the map."

"He's real but he's not legitimate," I said.

"You're sure?"

"Absolutely certain."

"That's very upsetting," Mr. Ready said unhappily but still smiling. "You try to function with integrity and the world passes you by."

"It does," I agreed. "It certainly does."

[76]

Chapter 6

"We want two Xerox copies of the questionnaires," Lucille told Mr. Ready.

"I'm afraid that's impossible. These are held in the strictest confidence."

"Ten dollars?"

"Far more confidential than that."

"Harvey, give Mr. Ready fifteen dollars, and that is as high as we go—the very last penny."

I took three five-dollar bills out of my pocket, and he had the copies made, and we went downstairs to the lobby, where I said to Lucille, "This has got to stop."

"What, Harvey?"

"You know damn well what. So go back to that damn Donnell branch of the New York Public Library where you belong."

"You don't mean that, Harvey."

"Now. I damn well do," I said fiercely.

"Oh, Harvey, you shouldn't talk tough, because it's like when that absolutely improbable fat man called you a shamus—"

"That's exactly what I mean," I said.

"What is exactly what you mean?"

"I mean you undercut my confidence. I mean you hit right to the heart of the whole problem of my masculinity. Do you think this is an easy world to be a man in? No, sir. Never."

"Harvey, I don't mean to."

"Maybe you don't mean to. That doesn't change the essential fact. How old are you?"

"Harvey, you know how old I am, and I think it's very humiliating for you to bring it up all the time."

"Very well. Twenty-nine years. And unmarried. Maybe that's why, and it's all very well to talk about humiliation, but how do you suppose I feel? I always wanted to be a film director and instead of that I'm an insurance dick, but I am supposed to be the smartest one in town. How do you think I feel? Do you know what you've been doing to me all day?"

"No, not really."

"Humiliating me."

"But I've been trying to help you," she said, quite horrified.

"You know how you could help me? Go back to your job."

"Harvey, I am on sick leave, and you know that I do care for you, and I am only trying to help a little, and it's just utterly insane to imagine that I have one tenth of your understanding and know-how, and I don't see what harm it does if I trail along—"

"Look, kid," I said to her, trying to be kind and understanding, "I know how you feel, but this can be a very dangerous job, and you have to keep on it. We should be at the Ritzhampton right now."

"But of course they're gone, Harvey, so there's no need to rush."

[78]

"How do you know they're gone?"

"Just because it's the most obvious thing in the world, Harvey, and if you—"

"I stared at her, and she swallowed her words and said, "All right Harvey. We go to the Ritzhampton, right now, and I apologize and I am sorry, and please don't make me go away because I am having more fun than I ever had since I was a little girl and I put my little sister Stephanie's yellow braids into black ink while she was sleeping—"

"You did that?"

"Yes."

"Why?"

"Because I hated Stephanie."

"Why did you hate her?"

"Because she was so damn good."

"Come along," I said, and we walked up Madison to the Ritzhampton. I half-suspected that they were one of the company's clients and when a phone call confirmed that they were, I introduced myself and Lucille to Mike Jacoby, the hotel security officer.

There is nothing very colorful about Mike Jacoby, who took his courses in police-psychology, criminology and hotel management at New York University; except that for a city boy who was born in the Bronx, he has covered himself with a remarkable veneer of international cool. He also has a mustache and has his suits made to order. He was very cooperative—perhaps because he couldn't take his eyes off Lucille—and he dug up the count's registration in a matter of minutes.

While I was looking at it, he whispered into my ear, "What's her name?"

"Cynthia Brandon."

"Not her. The gal you're with."

[79]

"Lucille Dempsey."

"You in love with her?"

"Why, what the hell has that got to do with anything?"

"I just asked a civil question. I want to know how deeply you are involved."

"Why?" I demanded. I had passed the registration card over to Lucille, who was studying it carefully now. Then she took the file and began to go through it. Jacoby stared at her as if he had never seen a woman before.

"Because I want to marry her."

"Just like that? You never met her before, but you want to marry her."

"If I had met her before, I would have married her. I been waiting for a woman like that."

"I'll ask her," I said.

"Just be careful how you put it."

"Lucille," I said, "Mr. Jacoby here, he thinks he is immediately in love with you and he wants to know whether you will marry him?"

"No," she replied. "But thank you, Mr. Jacoby. You know, there are two registrations for Count Gambion. And it's funny," she said to me, "that here this fellow registers openly at this hotel and your Lieutenant Rothschild and that clever Sergeant Kelly you were telling me about, they don't appear to know one blessed thing about it. Do they?"

"I guess not," I agreed.

"I would call that pretty poor police work, wouldn't you, Mr. Jacoby."

"You mean you would not even think of me in terms of marriage? Flatly—just like that?"

"Yes, but you musn't take offense. I mean, if we ran a branch of the Library System the way the police department seems to operate, we would never know where any book was."

"Lucille," I said. "The police department had no reason to inquire here—"

"The first one," Lucille said, "is for the Presidential suite. What about that, Mr. Jacoby?"

"Well, it's an excellent accommodation. You have no feeling about me?"

"We'll talk about that some time. How large, Mr. Jacoby?"

"Dining room, living room, three bedrooms, kitchen, pantry."

"How much?"

"Four hundred dollars a day."

"Oh, no. I don't believe it."

"Oh, it's not unreasonable. In the Carlyle, I believe they get even—"

"For crying out loud, Lucille," I began, but she went on smoothly, "And it never made you suspicious? A Count Gambion de Fonti appears and is able to pay that kind of ridiculous price for a few furnished rooms?"

"My dear Miss Dempsey," Jacoby said, "we only get suspicious when they don't pay. Really, you look at the whole matter rather oddly, if I may say so."

"Or sensibly. It's all a matter of one's point of view, isn't it. Now here on this second card, he registers as Count Gambion de Fonti and wife—for the Bridal Suite. Why did he have to register again?"

"That's a rule of the house."

"Let me see that!" I exclaimed. It was dated on Monday, exactly one week ago.

"And how much is the Bridal Suite?"

"Lucille, what difference does it make?"

[81]

"I should think it would make a difference, and even if it doesn't there's such a thing as a normal curiosity by someone who has a normal desire to be a bride even if not on these premises in this particular Bridal Suite."

"Three hundred and sixty dollars a day," said Jacoby. "Why should I be suspicious?"

"What on earth would you do with a girl like this?" I asked him.

"I'd figure something out. No, excuse me, Miss Dempsey. I don't mean it just that way, and he's cockeyed when he says I have fallen in love with you at first sight. All I mean is that I would like an opportunity to know you better."

"The name Cynthia Brandon rang no bells, did it, Jacoby?"

"Should it?"

"No. Not at all. She only happens to be the daughter of one of the richest men in America, namely E.C. Brandon."

"Elmer Cantwell Brandon?"

"That's right."

"Well, she certainly got married quietly," Jacoby said.

"You mean they actually lived here—in the Bridal Suite?" Lucille exclaimed.

"Overnight anyway."

"And then?"

"They checked out."

"Well, of course they checked out," Lucille said matter of factly.

We went into the records for a forwarding address, but there was none. We questioned the doorman, and out of him we squeezed the probability that they took a cab to Kennedy Airport. He was not sure. Almost sure, but not quite.

"Just who is this Count Gambion de Fonti?" Jacoby wanted to know.

[82]

"He's a hoodlum," I said, "so if you get any wind of him whatsoever let me know."

Then he tried to date Lucille again, and finally she gave him her telephone number. As we walked away from the hotel, I asked her, "Now, why on earth did you do that?"

"He was so insistent."

"He's a jerk."

"Then you have nothing to worry about, Harvey."

"Who's worried?"

"You're angry."

"I'm not angry—I'm just a little edgy about having you trailing all over the place with me."

"Do you want me to go, Harvey?"

"At this point, what I want seems to be absolutely academic."

"Anyway," she said, "I like your job. It's more fun than mine. I mean, it's just so lovely to have a job where there isn't a stitch of work to do and your time is absolutely your own."

"Now what do you mean by that?"

"Harvey, you're angry again."

"Work—my God, I work my butt off for that lousy insurance company."

"Of course you do, Harvey," she said.

Chapter 7

It was about three o'clock now, and the month of March, with its talent for idiotic whimsy, had decided upon spring. The sun was shining and the lightest, softest breeze was blowing from the south. There is a legend that London has the worst weather in the Western world, but the legend persists only because New Yorkers are not naturally boastful. So when such a day as this appears, the air sweet and clean, the sky blue and the temperature at a reasonable level, the city becomes absolutely gentle and worshipful with astonishment. I found myself holding hands with Lucille Dempsey.

"Harvey," she said, "let's go to the Zoo."

"What!"

"I know. You're thinking about what I said before. It wasn't a nice thing to say, was it, Harvey?"

"And the fact that I got a job to do?" I let go of her hand as if it were a hot poker.

"Harvey," she said reproachfully. "It was so nice to hold hands. I know you blame me for the entire Protestant ethic—which can be so nicely summed up as he who works is good and he who idles is bad. But there is another me."

"Where?"

"Just take my hand again and see. Also, isn't thinking the largest part of your job?"

I admitted that was so, and we walked to the Zoo. The notion that it would be a pleasant place on that Monday afternoon must have occurred to most of the population of mid-Manhattan, because the people outnumbered the animals at least twenty to one. Everyone has his own preference at the Central Park Zoo. Lucille was a sea-lion buff. I was always torn between the yak and the elephants—perhaps because the lugubrious touches me more deeply than anything else, and if there is anything more lugubrious than an elephant, it is a yak. She understood my point of view and we were holding hands again, and after we had viewed the elephants we went to the cafeteria for coffee.

"Harvey," Lucille said, "this is the nicest date we ever had."

I nodded.

"Also, you are relaxed, and that's very good. But, you know, this is practically the only date we ever had, except for those awful lunches you always buy me."

"How about twice to the Metropolitan Opera House?"

"If you call opera a date. Isn't it more like an obligation, Harvey? But there I am being nasty again, aren't I?"

"That's OK. I feel benign right now. Why did you want copies of the questionnaires?"

"Of course—I forgot all about that. Because something in it is very wrong. You realize why he married her, Harvey, don't you?"

"The citizenship thing. But just how does it work?"

"I think that calls for a lawyer, but in these questionnaires —here's what I want. I just saw it out of the corner of my eyes. It's in the section entitled *Character Analysis in Depth*, and it gives a list of thirty questions which are to be answered true or false. Now look at question twenty-one in the Count's folder. Quote—*In any group, I must be the leader*. Answer: *False*. Quote—*I prefer power to love*. Answer. *False*. That's question twenty-four. Now look at question twenty-nine. *I am satisfied with very little*. Answer. *True*." She glanced up at me curiously. "I don't know too much about this Mafia of yours, but it does seem to me that they found a wrongo to take over."

"Why should you think he answered the questions truthfully?"

"I just think he did."

"Why?"

"Why not?"

"Because a guy like this Corsica has characters all around him. Whatever he does, they do for him."

"Harvey, aren't you guessing as much as I am?"

"Maybe. But good God, he's supposed to take over the Syndicate."

"Where is that lawyer you mentioned before, Harvey?" she said primly. "I think we've loafed enough, don't you?"

"His name is Max Oppenheim, and he helped me through the divorce and he's very smart."

Oppenheim, Farrell and Adams are at 48th and Park Avenue, so we took a cab. It was about four-thirty in the afternoon when we got there and were ushered into Max Oppenheim's office, where he was having a little refreshment, namely three or four Danish pastries and a cup of coffee. He is a small man, about five feet and four inches, but what he lacks in height, he makes up in breadth. His suits are wonders of engineering, and strangely enough his two hundred and twenty pounds are not unbecoming. He begged us to have some Danish, and when we refused, he said that his partner, Joey Adams, did not have the same weight problem and therefore ate Napoleons and French doughnuts, and there were always one or two extra.

We both shook our heads, and Max said, "You know, Harvey, the trouble with skinny people is not simply the act of confronting you with their own svelt selves but the act of refusing goodies. It puts me down. It puts me down terribly."

Lucille thereupon had a piece of Danish, and Max observed, "This, Harvey, is a kind girl. She's got heart and compassion. Do you want to marry her? You're free to. Unless you married that Sarah Cotter who was mixed up in the Sabin case."

"He did not," Lucille said. "Harvey may be a fink, but he is not stupid."

"Mostly not. Then what can I do for you?"

"We got a hypothetical case," I told him, "but it's very important Max, so I don't want you to think I am just wasting your time."

"I charge you anyway, Harvey, so what's the difference?"

"But, Max, this is only a hypothetical case."

"Harvey, you come for advice. I sell advice, and it's only hypothetical because it's maybe somewhat illegal. I ought to charge you double."

"You wouldn't."

"I wouldn't. Anyway, it goes into expenses."

"It still hurts Harvey. You have to understand that," Lucille said sweetly.

"I understand," Max said.

"All right, you've had your fun. Here's the case. A man enters the United States, legally but under a phony name, so

[88]

that means he has forged papers. He needs citizenship but his papers and background won't stand up, so he needs an extra prop. We think that in order to get this extra prop, he married an American girl, but we are very hazy on procedure."

"You think he married the girl? Or did he actually marry her?"

"He married her."

"That is, we're practically certain," Lucille put in. "We have no evidence that the marriage actually took place."

"It would seem that they shared a connubial bed," I said.

"Isn't that a wonderful word, Harvey," Max said eagerly. "Connubial. That's a real lawyer word. Why don't you ask them?"

"Who?"

"The newlyweds."

"Because they cleared out."

"No forwarding address?"

"None."

"Any other plausible reasons for the marriage? I mean beside this citizenship thing?"

"No—"

"There is always the possibility that they were in love," Lucille said, and I told her, "Honey—come off it."

"Well, you don't believe in love, Harvey. You know you don't."

"Oh, Harvey's had his moments," Max said in my defense.

"I suppose so. With that dreadful person you divorced him from."

"She wasn't that dreadful," I protested.

"Nor did I divorce him from her," Max said in his own defense. "The judge did that. All I did was to make sure that Harvey came out of the grinder wearing his clothes. Now

[89]

look, kids—get back to this. You want me to create a presumptive course of action for your male partner in said hypothetical case."

"You put that so nicely," Lucille said.

"Thank you. All right. I take the few facts as you give them to me. This man wants permanent entry. He wants to establish a position of residence with rights that would be stronger and quicker than the regular procedure that an immigrant must go through. By the way—this American girl—born here?"

"Right."

"How did he get to her, if I may ask."

"Does that figure?"

"It just might."

"Well, he and the girl both filled out questionnaires for computer dating?"

"What?"

"You know," Lucille smiled. "IBM machines and all that."

"I have no idea what you're talking about."

"Oh, come on Max—everyone's heard about this."

"I haven't."

"Well, it's very big with college kids and I suppose in some high schools and around certain adults. They—these dating firms—get out a set of questionnaires with spaces for all kinds of information about yourself. You know—what do you know about sex, how old are you, what color are your eyes, do you like Tom Courtney better than Burt Lancaster?"

"That's the way it's done today?" Max asked incredulously.

"It's more of a tomorrow business," Lucille said. "You know—the shadow of the future. Everyone has a number and the numbers are fed into great computers—all that sort of horror stuff."

"You're absolutely putting me on," Max said, "and it is certainly not a very friendly thing to do to a successful overweight lawyer."

"No, Max," I explained. "Unfortunately, that's the way the truth runs these days. And it's a very simple computer problem. The computer is programmed to pair the questionnaires with the highest number of similar and complementary replies. The cockeyed theory is that if you like strawberry shortcake and I like strawberry shortcake and we both smoke pot, we can live happily ever after."

"It seems extremely unlikely," Max said. "I have a wife and five children, Harvey. Did you know that divorce is quite rare in families of five children and more. A good deal of desertion but very little divorce. All right, so these two characters met in a computer. We presume they are married. You want to know what their next step is?"

"That's right."

"They go to Canada."

"Why to Canada?" Lucille demanded.

"You're a nice girl," Max said, "but you are very quick to take umbrage, as they say. Maybe the only logic in it is that they should go to Canada."

"I can't see that."

"Of course not, because you don't know immigration law. I'm no expert on it, but I know what the logical procedure is. Your man now has an American wife, but that by no means makes him an American citizen, nor does it guarantee him any permanent residence in this country."

"But I thought—"

"Naturally. So does everyone else—marry an American girl and you have it made. But that's just a step. Is this hypothetical man of yours an idiot or is he well-advised?"

[91]

"He's well-advised," replied.

"Then he knows what steps to take. One—he married the girl. Two—he goes to Canada. Three—in Canada, he goes to the American Consulate or Immigration Office and applies for a visa for permanent entry, on grounds that he has married an American citizen. Barring unusual circumstances, such a visa will be granted."

"So that's how it's done," Lucille said.

"That's exactly how it's done."

"It seems silly."

There was a long silence, and then Max said, "You're right. It does seem silly. But that is how it's done."

"But you see," said Lucille, "it's really not very much good to us unless we know where he went in Canada."

"Lucille, how on earth is Max supposed to know where he went?"

"Maybe I do."

Now we both stared at Max.

"What do you mean, maybe you do?"

"You say he is well-advised?"

"That's a good presumption."

"Then it is an equally sound presumption to say that he went to Toronto."

"Why?"

"You know, Harvey, if all of my clients were like you, I would go out of my mind. A lawyer is like a doctor. Do you ask your doctor why?"

"I do," Lucille said.

"Sure you do. It figures. But does Harvey?"

"I only go to an analyst," I said. "Can you ask an analyst why? You know what my analyst says when I ask him why?"

"No, I don't know."

"He says I am a nut. OK, let us not get hung up on this. He goes to Toronto."

"For some good reasons, Harvey," Max said earnestly. "Since Montreal and Quebec and Halifax are all seaports, they have more specific immigration problems and answers, too. If your man is hot, as you lead me to suspect, he will go inland. The Consulate in Toronto is somewhat easier, and American Airlines has a new jet that gets you there in forty-five minutes."

"I don't know—" I said dubiously.

"Well, it's your baby, Harvey, so kick it around as you see fit. My brains are picked. You will get a bill at the end of the month. You going to marry her?" he asked, nodding at Lucille.

"You know I'm not in any condition to get married."

"It upsets Harvey when you talk about marriage. As his lawyer, you ought to know that."

"You're a smart girl," Max said. "My advice is very simple. Put a little pressure in the right place and it's got to give."

"Let's go," I said to Lucille.

I got up and went to the door, and Max called after me, "Harvey!"

I held the door open for Lucille.

"Harvey—a little advice on the house."

"I'm waiting," I said.

"Call the cops, Harvey."

"What?"

"Call in the cops, Harvey. They get paid to clean up."

"Thanks," I said.

"Keep an eye on him," he said to Lucille.

Chapter 8

Down in the street, the golden haze of the afternoon was washing into the murky twilight of New York, and the glass-hung buildings were pouring out their millions for the evening rush homeward. In another hour would come the best time the city knows, the streets cool and empty, rather forlorn and still echoing to the turmoil of the day but quieting and full of increasing hush. Only the New Yorker who lives in Midtown can savor that quiet and properly know it. But, now, and for the next forty minutes or so, the streets were like rivers of people, and I stood there for a moment in the midst of it with Lucille, thinking that we had spent the best part of a day together and that it hadn't been half-bad, allowing for her tendency to combine the roles of mother, dictator, teacher and interpreter. All in all, we had gotten along quite well, and I felt that I owed her an apology of sorts, and I told her straightforwardly that it had been a very good day indeed.

"I mean, I really enjoyed it, Lucille. Oh, I might have snapped at you once or twice—"

"Not really, Harvey."

[95]

"But that's my neurotic problem, not yours."

"Of course, Harvey."

"And now I have a million things to do and all sorts of pieces to tie together," I told her gently, "and I have to find out when the next jet leaves and get out to Kennedy—"

"LaGuardia," Lucille interrupted, just as gently.

"What do you mean, LaGuardia?"

"I mean that we have to get to LaGuardia not to Kennedy. The jet leaves from LaGuardia. It's American Airlines. There was one at five but we missed that. There is another at seven and we have plenty of time to make that one, and that will get us to Toronto at eight-thirteen."

"Max said forty-five minutes," I said lamely.

"Did he? Well, that's a sort of exaggeration. Oh, I suppose that if we have tailwinds we can make it in less than an hour, but it is scheduled for one hour and thirteen minutes."

"How do you know?"

"I asked Max's secretary to find out."

"When?"

"When you were arguing with Max."

"Well, I never saw you leave the room."

"Because the door was open, Harvey, and I simply stepped through and whispered to her."

"You're always whispering. You know, that's a sneaky habit."

"What a thing to say!"

"And just what did you mean when you said that *we* have to get out to LaGuardia?"

"Harvey, you're becoming truculent."

"I am not becoming truculent. I am perfectly calm. We have had a good day. You've been a good sport. I like you. You tend to dominate everything that comes your way, but I like you anyway. I suppose I am the kind of non-hero type that needs some kind of domination, so I am not complaining. But right now I have to go to Toronto—alone!"

"And you'd leave me here. After running through this maze all day, now, when it first becomes interesting, you'd leave me here. I don't believe it, Harvey. I just don't believe you're that kind of person."

She got a handkerchief out of her purse and began to dab at her eyes, and I said coldly, "Put it away. The tears are phony. Suppose you just tell me exactly what you want."

"All right. I never had so much fun in my life. I want to go with you."

"No."

"Yes."

"Do you know how long it would take you to go home and pack and get ready?"

"I'm ready right now. One hour and thirteen minutes. It's like going to Brooklyn, Harvey."

"No!"

And then we argued for ten minutes, and then it took another fifteen minutes to get a cab to take us out to La-Guardia. We had time for a sandwich at the airport, and there were a few goodies with the cocktails on the flight. The jet went up and went down, and at 8:09 P. M., four minutes ahead of schedule, the plane touched the ground at Malton Airport in Toronto. It was then and only then that for some idiotic reason Lucille realized that we were in another country, without luggage, and—at least as far as she was concerned —with very limited funds. I told her, as we walked through the terminal, that she owed me $54.60.

"What?"

"Well, I bought two round-trip tickets. That's what the game costs—$54.60 each. You said you wanted to play."

"Harvey, do you mean to say that with your pockets stuffed

[97]

with expense money, you're going to hold me up for that ticket?" She opened her purse and rummaged through it. "Anyway, I only have $12.27. So either you'll have to trust me or take a check—if you just have the nerve to come right out and be chintzy enough to take a check."

"Suppose we have to stay overnight?"

"Harvey," she said sweetly, "where is the return section of my round-trip ticket?"

I gave it to her and she tucked it into her purse, and then she swung around and marched off in the opposite direction, toward American Airlines reservations.

"Lucille, where are you off to?" I called after her.

"Back to New York. You'll get my check in the mail."

"Don't be a nut." She kept on and I ran after her and caught up to her at the reservations desk, and I grabbed her arm and said, "Look, I trust you. Let's forget the whole thing."

"Take your hand off my arm, sir," she said coldly.

"So I goofed."

"So you are the chintziest, cheapest man I have ever known, Harvey Krim, and the only reason I abide you is out of a misplaced sense of pity."

The girl behind the reservations counter was following all of this with great interest. "We all come up against the same thing," she offered.

"What do you mean, we all come up against the same thing?"

"When does the next plane for New York leave?" Lucille demanded.

"The male market is lousy. In about forty minutes, Miss."

"Do you want me to get down on my knees?" I asked Lucille.

"Yes."

"I am on my knees," I said.

"You are not. But I will accept the apology, and you are not to mention money to me again while we are in Canada—do you understand, Harvey?"

"I understand," I said.

"Good. Now let's get a cab to the Prince York Hotel."

I went along with her, and I didn't ask her why the Prince York until we were in the cab and on our way. "You know, if we were married," I began, and then I saw her face, full of understanding and patience, and I said, "The hell with that. Fred Bronstein would bust a gut laughing. What do you mean, the Prince York Hotel?"

"Who's Fred Bronstein?"

"My analyst."

"Well, what right has he to laugh?"

"Why is it the Prince York Hotel?"

"Because that's the biggest hotel in Toronto, and it also just happens to be the biggest hotel in the world."

"You really pull no punches. Now it's the biggest hotel in the world, only they misplaced it in Toronto, Canada."

"Ask the driver, Harvey," Lucille said sweetly.

"Jack," I said to the driver, "how about it? Is it the biggest hotel or isn't it?"

"First, I am not crazy about Yanks. Second, my name ain't Jack. Third, I got you for the five miles from the airport to the hotel but I ain't no information center. The dame's right."

"What do you mean, you don't like Americans?" Lucille asked.

"Look, lady, I don't want an argument. I told the man you were right. It's the biggest hotel in the world."

[99]

"Where else would he go?" Lucille whispered to me.

"There are other hotels in Toronto."

"Wouldn't he want the biggest?"

"Maybe she wouldn't."

"Why on earth should he listen to her?" Lucille asked.

"Ah."

"What does that mean? 'Ah.'"

So it went, until finally we were at the Prince York. If it was not the biggest hotel in the world, it came close to it. Lucille asked what we should say if they questioned our lack of luggage, and I assured her that they would not question it. "A thousand people walk in and out of here every hour," I told her.

"But they don't register."

"And what makes you think we're going to register?" I asked, looking at her strangely.

"Well, it's eight-thirty, Harvey, and here we are in Toronto—oh, don't look at me like that, Harvey. You're a big boy and I am a big girl, and I've never been to Canada before. I understand that you can buy the most marvelous British sweaters here, and I want to do some sightseeing, and—"

"And we will be on a plane back to New York tonight."

"I thought you came here to find your Cynthia?"

"Maybe. And maybe the loving couple has been in and out as fast as I intend for us to be."

"Well, I might as well tell you," Lucille said smugly, "that the last plane out of here for New York leaves at nine-thirty, and it's ten minutes to nine right now."

If she said, it was so. I ended the argument and suggested that she do her shopping in the enormous lobby while I found the hotel security officer.

"Without me?"

"Without you," I said firmly.

"All right, Harvey," she agreed. "You know I am not going to argue one bit, because I'm sure they checked out, just as you said, and would you like me to call the American Consulate?"

"What for?"

"They would have to go there for their visas. That's what your friend Max said."

"They'll be closed up at this hour."

"Can I try, Harvey?"

I humored her and said that she could try, and we arranged to meet in that part of the lobby facing the registration desk. The young lady at the desk told me that the security officer of the hotel was one Captain Albert Gustin, and when I let her know that I was a private investigator, she informed me that Captain Gustin had been with Scotland Yard; and that right now he was probably not in his office; but that I could try.

"You know, we get a lot of international trade here, and if there is anything I can do for you, Mr. Krim—that was not your wife, was it?"

"Oh, no—no."

"I think it is absolutely fascinating for a young, unmarried man to travel with his secretary. Or are you married, Mr. Krim?"

"No."

"Oh?"

"She's not my secretary."

"Oh." She thought about it for a while, and then she said, "Do you want a double? If you have no luggage, the rule of the house is that you must pay in advance. It's such a silly, old-fashioned rule, isn't it?"

I took two singles, paying for them in advance and wondering how I had ever gotten into this situation and recollecting that the only reason I was here at all was firstly because of the guess of a fat lawyer and secondly because of the guess of an insane librarian.

At the security office, at the other end of the vast, palm-fronded, Egyptian decor lobby, I had the good luck to find Captain Gustin after all. He wore tweeds, smoked a pipe, looked like John Wayne, spoke with an English accent, and had three mirrors spotted around his office, so that there was never a moment when he couldn't see himself merely by moving his eyeballs. He explained that he happened to be available at this hour because he had a dinner date at the hotel, and when he touched his hair affectionately, I realized that he also wore a toupé. He was at least six foot-three inches, and I am not at my best with very large men. When we shook hands, the pain was only just bearable.

"Harvey Krim," he said, looking at my card. "You know, there are chaps like you at Lloyds, aren't there? Get back the loot and all that. Pay off the crooks. I'm not sure I approve of any of it."

"We're almost as large as Lloyds," I said, hoping to impress him.

He examined his lower face in a mirror and told me that I had no authority to speak of north of the border.

"I don't have much south of the border, either," trying the open and frank approach.

"Well, now—there you are. No fuss, and we shall get along quite well." He looked at his watch. "Lovely little bird. They're to ring me from the desk when she appears. Married man, Krim?"

"Divorced."

[102]

"Ah. Puts us in the same case, doesn't it? I hear you're traveling with delicious baggage. All for it."

I thanked God that I was not large and aggressive, because if I were large and aggressive, I would have belted him and probably ended up in a Canadian can.

"Now what's your kick, Krim?"

He mixed his slang and his metaphors. I told him what my kick was.

"Nonsense. Don't believe a word of it."

"What do you mean, you don't believe a word of it?"

"Guesswork and romantic nonsense. Mafia! Haw! Utter nonsense. No such thing as the Mafia. You Yanks love your bit of adventure. Can't stand to confess that you're ridden with gangsters, so you push this Mafia bit."

"You mean there's no Mafia then?"

"Absolutely."

"I invented it?"

"Not at all, Krim. For heaven's sake, don't take umbrage. You go along with the crowd."

"I weigh one fifty-three, stripped," I said.

"Oh? Not really in shape at all, are you. Good regular workouts would be a cure for that."

"Did I also invent Valento Corsica, alias Count Gambion de Fonti?"

"Come now, Krim," he said. "You are peeved, aren't you? Kind of indicating that if I were your weight, we might get along differently. Not at all. I consider you the best of good fellows. Let me put the matter to rest." He picked up the telephone, and said into it, "Gustin here. Go over our files on registration for the past ten days and see whether you can't come up with a Valento Corsica or a Count Gambion de Fonti—" He turned back to me, "How do you spell those foul

[103]

names, Krim?" I told him, and as he listened he spoke into the phone and watched himself in the mirror simultaneously. He had gifts, no doubt about it. "That's the good chap," he said into the phone; and while I never pretended to be a Henry Higgins, I decided on the moment that he was no more British than I was. He put down the phone. "Won't take but a minute or two."

I thanked him. "Good of you to cooperate."

"Not at all. Like Toronto?"

"Well, since I have been here less than two hours, and practically all of it spent in a cab and in this hotel, I'm not in any position to say."

"Good. Good. You chaps do have a sense of humor."

"I'm pleased to hear that," I said. "But I don't think your man will find either of those names on the register."

"Why not? You said he married under the name of de Fonti."

"Did I? But even if that is the case, he'd have no trouble convincing his bride that a count should travel incognito."

"Aren't you stretching the point, old chap? I am sure that if Count Gamby or whatever the devil his name is should come to the hotel, he would register properly. Why not?"

"I told you about the Mafia," I explained patiently and politely.

"There you go again." The phone rang, and he picked it up and said, "Right. Right. Right. Right. Shan't be a moment." Back with the telephone, and he explained to me, "No names, not here—not at all. Afraid you've had a wild goose chase for it, old chap. Wish I could take you into the bar for a couple, but the bird is here. Do come and take a peep at her."

"Aren't you at least going to check on how many couples of

[104]

fit age and appearance registered here? Description? Accent?
We could talk to the desk clerks—"

"My dear chap," he said, "you do take yourself seriously.
But you are not a member of Interpol or even of the New
York City Police. We can't turn the house upside down for
you. It is the biggest hotel in the world."

I followed him out of the room to where the "bird"
waited. She was a bleached blonde in her forties with two
important recommendations—a size forty bust and height.
John Wayne licked his lips over her as if he had never seen a
woman before, and they waltzed out of there in great style.
He didn't bother to say goodby to me.

I occupied a chair facing the desk, and I waited and waited.
I got the local papers and the evening papers from New York,
and I waited again. I read Walter Lippman, James Reston
and Max Lerner, discovered that the world was both a sorry
mess and a very sex-ridden place, and I waited some more.

I went to the desk and asked about a message.

"I'll look in your box, Mr. Krim. Shall I also look in Miss
Dempsey's box?"

No messages.

I returned to the chair and waited. A member of John
Wayne's security force approached me and asked whether he
had not seen me before?

"Sure. You saw me in Gustin's office. You were sitting in
the front room, typing. I'm an insurance investigator. My
name is Harvey Krim."

"Got it. Anything I can do for you, Mr. Krim?"

"When does the American Consulate close?"

"Who knows? Five, six, seven—sometimes they work later,
I suppose. They're closed now, of course."

I thanked him and I waited. It became ten o'clock and

then eleven o'clock. The movement in the lobby died away. I could have gone up to the room I had paid for, but by now I was too nervous, too frightened to leave the lobby. Instead, I reviewed in my mind all the things that could happen to a decent girl I had dragged into this mess with the Mafia—a simple, uncomplicated girl who lived her life among books and had nothing to do with this corrupt and dirty piece of mankind that constituted my business affiliation and area of work. Of course it was all my fault. I even decided that Gustin could be one of them. Then he'd go after the girl, which was quite obviously my Achilles' heel. Maybe she had a mother. They'd fish her up out of the river, and out of common courtesy, I would have to bring the news to her mother. Funny, but I had never asked Lucille about her mother. What would I say? That Lucille adored me, and for that reason I had lost her in a foreign city?

It was just ten minutes past midnight when I found her. She came walking into the hotel, clinging to the arm of a man who was at least ten years younger than I—which meant younger than she—and a good deal better looking, if you like the superficial, so-called clean cut-American-boy type. Half a block away, on the other side of the lobby, they stretched their parting to at least five minutes, and then he leaned over and kissed her cheek. And when she got to where I was she had the gall to say, "Poor Harvey. You look so tired and worried."

"You don't. You look as fresh as a Goddamn rose."

"Harvey!"

"And who was that?"

"Harvey, I do believe that you're jealous," she said, smiling with pleasure. "That's so nice, Harvey. But it's nothing to get jealous about. Jimmy's a nice boy, lovely boy—

Harvard, and it was such wonderful fun to talk about old days at the Yard—but that's just what he is, a very pleasant boy."

"Which is undoubtedly why you felt it your duty to kiss him."

"That? Oh, Harvey, that wasn't a kiss at all. It was a little bit of a sibling peck on the cheek. Oh, do stand up." I stood up, and she put her arms around me and kissed me on the lips. "That, Harvey, is a real kiss—a gentle one but real. Do you feel better now?"

"Why should I feel better? Do you know what I kept thinking sitting here?"

"No."

"That you had been knocked over or strangled or something—"

"Harvey, how sweet! And all I was doing was having dinner with a nice boy who works in the Consulate."

"Dinner? You mean to say you went off and had dinner and left me here to starve?"

"Harvey, what else was I to do? I called the Consulate, and the only one there except the cleaning woman was Jimmy, who had stayed to catch up on his work, and we sort of met over the phone, and when he learned that I was Radcliffe, 1960—he's Harvard, 1963—and I never lie about my age, as you know, Harvey, well, he insisted that I come over to the Consulate, and then he insisted that I have dinner with him, because he's not married and this is only his second month in Toronto, and he is terribly lonely, even though he's the first assistant to the vice-consul—is that right? Are there vice-consuls?

"How the devil should I know whether there are vice-consuls?"

"Please don't be angry, Harvey, because I did find out what you wanted to know—I mean about Cynthia and the count."

"You did?"

"Oh, yes—yes, indeed, Harvey. They got their visas today and left for New York this evening on the seven o'clock."

"How do you know?"

"Their visas were validated at the airport, so there you are. We must have passed them in midair."

"And of course they stayed at the Prince York," I said.

"You're so grumpy, Harvey—you're not even grateful. No, they did not stay at the Prince York. No one does anymore. They stayed at the Regency, which is the poshest new hotel here."

Chapter 9

At first, I thought it was Sergeant Kelly, and I said to Lucille, "You see that one over there, the big feller with the dark hair and the tweeds, he's a dead ringer for this Sergeant Kelly who holds Rothschild up, so that Rothschild can hate me better than if he had to hold himself up at the same time."

Then it turned out to be Sergeant Kelly, which proved at least that I was not becoming more paranoid than usual. He was standing in front of the information counter at Malton Terminal, and next to him was a thick-necked, burly man who had fuzz woven in and out of his clothing. Kelly grinned at me and called out,

"Over here, Harvey. Good to see a friendly face in a strange land."

"Then it is Sergeant Kelly!" Lucille exclaimed with delight.

"And this is my colleague, Constable Brimpton, of the Toronto police. Shake hands with Harvey Krim, Constable Brimpton."

Handcrushers were evidently endemic to Toronto. Finally,

Constable Brimpton let go of my hand, smiled upon me with approval, and then nodded to Kelly.

"You were right, Sergeant," he said to Kelly; and then to me, "Clever lad. Harvey Krim—clever lad. You have a reputation well deserved. A bit agile on occasion, as Kelly tells me, but clever."

It was ten minutes after nine on the following morning, and we were on our way through the terminal at Malton to get our plane, and there they were. I thanked them both.

"And this will be Cynthia Brandon, of course," Constable Brimpton said. "Well, it's not for me to be critical of the way they do things in the States, but I always say, spare the rod and spoil the child."

"You always say that?" Lucille asked.

"I do indeed, Miss Brandon."

"She's not Miss Brandon," I said.

"Harvey!"

"Now look, Sergeant," I said to him, "we are not in New York. We are not even in the United States. We are in the Dominion of Canada, and here in the Dominion—oh, the hell with all that! Go blow your horn."

"You are forgetting me, Mr. Krim," Constable Brimpton said sternly.

"How on earth did you know we were here?" Lucille asked, fascinated.

"Feller called Gustin put it on the wire at the Toronto police headquarters. All points. Lieutenant Rothschild had me take the first plane this morning. We been waiting here."

"Lousy John Wayne creep," I said.

"It's utterly delicious," Lucille said. "But I am not Cynthia Brandon."

"Of course you are."

[110]

Constable Brimpton supported that. "Now see here, Missy," he said, "arguments make things unpleasant and we don't want any arguments, do we, Missy?"

"What did you call me?" Lucille asked coldly.

"Missy."

"Well, don't you ever dare call me that again. Not ever! And both of you listen to me. My name is Lucille Dempsey, and I work at the Donnell Branch of the New York Public Library. Have you ever heard of the New York Public Library? I have heard of Expo '67."

"Now, Missy, we don't want to drag Expo '67 into this, do we?"

"Missy! How dare you!"

That was beyond me; that was deep inside of a new Lucille, and I turned it back to reality by telling Kelly, "She just happens to be telling the truth. How old is Cynthia Brandon?"

"Twenty."

"All right, take a good look at my friend, Miss Dempsey. Does she look twenty?"

Kelly stared at her.

"You've seen pictures of the Brandon kid."

"I guess I have," Kelly said slowly.

Her face white and angry, Lucille opened her purse and took out a driver's license and other cards. Kelly looked at them, and then we were able to say a pleasant goodbye to Constable Brimpton. That is, I said the goodbye. Lucille said nothing.

When we went out toward the plane, Kelly walked with us. I assured him that it was not necessary.

"That's what Rothschild wants. The Lieutenant wants I should stick with you closer than glue."

[111]

"This isn't New York. It's not even the States. It's Canada."

"That's why I am being extra polite and delicate," Kelly replied.

His seat was close to the tail, about six rows behind us. I sat down next to Lucille, who had not said a word during the past fifteen minutes—which in Lucille was entirely out of character.

We fastened our seatbelts, and then I said that while Constable Brimpton may have touched a sore spot, it was unwitting.

"Not unwitting but witless, and not Constable Brimpton but you."

"Me?"

"You, Harvey Krim, are a louse."

"Me? Why? What have I done?"

"A brainless louse," she said.

"What? After all I did for you—after shelling out for this trip and a hotel room and—"

"Yes, sir, Harvey Krim, the last of the big spenders. The Great Gatsby. The last of the oldtime sports."

"If I had one notion of what I did—"

We were airborne and approaching altitude, which allowed Sergeant Kelly to unfasten his seatbelt, amble over to where we were, and ask Lucille whether they couldn't have a few words together.

"Blow," I said. "Miss Dempsey has nothing to say to you."

"Miss Dempsey will decide that," Lucille said primly, rising. "There is an empty seat next to you, isn't there, Sergeant?"

"There is indeed, Miss Dempsey."

Without giving me a second glance, Lucille went off with Kelly; and I may say that in my time I have been through a good deal of this and that, but this beat everything. The enormous effrontry of it was such that for a matter of minutes I simply sat frozen in my seat, and I suppose I looked the way I felt, because the stewardess stopped to ask me whether I was all right. "More or less," I said. "Tell me, Miss, how old are you? Or am I stepping out of line?"

"I'm dated tonight," she replied. "I'm twenty-four. I'm free day after tomorrow."

"Would you get angry if I said no one would mistake you for seventeen?"

She smiled and said she would be delighted. "Twenty is something else. I mean, who wants to be mistaken for seventeen, but my friends say I haven't changed an iota in the past four years. Oh, oh—there's my signal."

She left, and I sat motionless. Not entirely motionless; looked at from the rear, I tried to give the impression of being relaxed and casual; but I did not get up for the next ten minutes. That was as long as I could hold the pose. I went back to the tail and drew myself a drink of water. Kelly was on the outside seat; he had put Lucille inside, next to the window. I leaned over them, smiled, hoped they were having a good chat, and poured the glass of water into Kelly's tweed lap. I fussed and apologized all over the place, but it did not halt the natural reflex in Kelly, who leaped up, got me by the lapel, and whispered, "Goddamn little creep—I ought to break every bone in your body."

"Ah, now, Kelly," I said soothingly. "We are out of the city and in an airplane. Think of the headline—city cop slugs private eye in plane. Or better yet—city plainclothesman

[113]

crosses state line illegally and enters Canada. Oh, juicy. Rothschild would love that, wouldn't he?"

Mine was a return whisper. Lucille, seeing me in the grip of two hundred and ten pounds of bone and muscle, said to Kelly scathingly, "I misjudged you, sir. I certainly did."

He let go of me and turned to her.

"A simple accident and you're ready to kill a man," she said. "Do you ever think of anything but force and brutality —or is that your natural reaction?"

He let go of me and stared at her dumbly, mouth open, water dripping from his trousers. I went back to my seat, trying not to think of what might happen the next time I met Kelly in New York, and in a few minutes, Lucille joined me. As she sat down, she said, "Only one thing, Harvey Krim, and for once in your life tell the truth—did you deliberately empty a cup of water onto Sergeant Kelly?"

"Yes."

"Deliberately?"

"Yes."

"Do you know why? Or are you simply psychopathic about such things?"

"I don't like him."

"I only talked with him for a few minutes, but he appeared to be decent and forthright—and well-educated."

"That's exactly why I don't like him. He was probably so decent and forthright that you spilled everything. Right?"

"You can't like someone who's decent and forthright, can you?"

"Honey, let's not get off on that tack."

"Admit it," she pressed me.

"Well, I like *you*. As a matter of fact, there are times when I believe that I am a little bit nutty about you."

[114]

"Harvey—"

"And then you dominate me. First thing out of the bag. Look, just what did you tell Kelly?"

"Well, I really didn't tell him anything, Harvey. You know, what you said is very sweet. I don't think I dominate you. I just can't think of myself that way. I'm only a librarian, Harvey. And you shouldn't say that I spilled everything to Kelly. I didn't tell him about that enormous sum of money you are carrying."

"But?"

"He asked me whether I thought Cynthia was kidnapped. Well, it's hardly likely that a girl who goes around marrying prince-regents of the Mafia of her own free will is being kidnapped. You know, Jimmy said that was a lot of nonsense about the Mafia. He said that the Mafia is one great big myth and simply does not exist."

"Who the hell is Jimmy?"

"Harvey, you're jealous. Of course you remember Jimmy. He's the boy from the Consulate who bought me dinner. He's sweet and he's certainly no competition—"

"He's an idiot. What did you tell Kelly when he asked you whether you thought that Cynthia was kidnapped?"

"I told him what Jimmy said about there being no such thing as the Mafia."

"You told that to Kelly?"

"He didn't get grumpy like you. He just thought it was a good thing that nice boys like Jimmy were in the diplomatic service and not on the New York City Police Force, and he agreed that Cynthia was probably not kidnapped, and then I told him how Jimmy tracked her and the count at the Consulate."

"Oh, my God, no," I moaned. "You didn't tell him that?"

[115]

"Well, why not, Harvey? I mean, even if the Mafia is a myth, this fake count is playing footsie with the law, isn't he?"

"What else?"

"Nothing else. I only sat there a few minutes, and if you weren't stupid beyond the call of duty, I would not have been there at all."

"Me? Stupid?"

"Oh, Harvey—about women."

"Did you tell him about the Ritzhampton?"

She frowned and then shook her head. "I don't think I even mentioned that. Why?"

"Because I have a crazy notion that they went right back there."

"Who?"

"Corsica and Cynthia."

"No. They wouldn't do that."

"Why not?" I demanded. "They don't know they're being chased. They don't know that anyone has seen them. They don't look upon themselves as fugitives—"

"Harvey!" she burst out.

"What now?"

"Harvey, I forgot to tell you."

"What?"

"Something else Jimmy said."

"If Jimmy said it, I don't want to hear it."

"Oh, but you do, Harvey. You certainly do. Jimmy said that the count had no business marrying anyone except a boy."

"What?"

"That's right. The count likes boys, not girls."

"Well, how the hell would Jimmy know about that?"

[116]

She took a deep breath and said, "Because Jimmy looks like he is but he isn't."

"And just how do you know he isn't?"

"Because a girl can tell."

"That's a hell of a note!" I exclaimed indignantly.

"Oh, Harvey, you're a silly ass. You never made a real pass at me. You suffer from reverse Momism. That Cotter girl you almost married, she was thin as a stick. I always thought that 38-24-38 was a rather nice thing to walk around with, but—"

"You're 38-24-38?"

"Yes, Harvey."

"That's a hell of a thing for a librarian to be."

"The world changes, Harvey."

"But your friend, Jimmy, could be mistaken about the count—"

"No, he couldn't, Harvey. The count made a pass at Jimmy."

"He did? How? When?"

"When Cynthia went to the little girls' room, and the count was alone with Jimmy for about three minutes. No diddling, Harvey—but a real, honest-to-goodness pass."

I studied her curiously and with new interest. "You really have a rounded education. So that's the way it is. I just can't believe that they would ever pick one to lead the mob. That's what makes no sense. It makes no damn sense at all. Couldn't he be a switch-hitter?"

"That doesn't solve your problem, Harvey. You know what I think?"

"No, I don't know what you think."

"I think that if there is a Mafia like you say, then they're smart enough to know about other syndicates, like Fats Coventry's gang in Texas. And if they have a new boss, they

[117]

certainly don't want him turned into a target. So they ring in a decoy to draw the fire, and then they eliminate the threat of the opposition."

"That is the craziest proposition I ever heard of," I said.

"Just a notion, Harvey. Poor Cynthia."

"Let's just find her. The marriage can be annulled."

"Still, I say, poor Cynthia."

Chapter 10

It was quite early on Tuesday morning when we landed at LaGuardia, with Kelly tacked on to us like a glued label; and with Lucille still complaining that she could not understand why we did not throw in our lot with the cops.

"Because no one throws in with the cops. With the cops, you surrender."

"So we surrender, Harvey."

"Krim doesn't surrender," I answered grimly.

"For heaven's sake, Harvey," she said, "aren't they on our side? They want to find the girl too. So we help them."

"In the first place, you don't help cops except that you help them their way—"

"That's a most peculiar syntax, Harvey."

"What difference does it make? I'm trying to get a point across."

"If you don't think syntax makes a difference, Harvey, then we have lost the ability to communicate."

"All right. You run with hoodlums and your syntax suffers. Does that satisfy you? I apologize."

"Harvey!"

"All right. Let me put it to you bluntly. You have heard me complain about my boss, Alex Hunter, and about that ulcer-ridden monster over at the Nineteenth Precinct, Lieutenant Rothschild; but they are both little lambs compared to a Mr. Homer Smedly, who is the vice-president of the third largest insurance company in the world. People go around thinking—"

"Here's a cab, Harvey," she said.

We got into the cab, and Kelly got into one directly behind us. I took a ten-dollar bill out of my pocket and gave it to the driver, and said, "Here's the tip. I pay another five plus whatever's on the meter and we're going to the Ritz-hampton on Madison Avenue."

"Who do you want me to kill, mister?" the driver asked happily.

"That's your problem. See the olive-green job behind us?"

"I see."

"Can you lose him?"

"For ten bucks, Captain, I can lose J. Edgar Hoover and forty G-men. Rest easy."

We ripped out of the place, and Lucille reminded me that I had been telling her about Homer Smedly.

"Who runs the company," I said. "You know what an insurance company deals with? Money. You know what they like? Money. The aforesaid Homer Smedly handed me a check for fifteen thousand clams, and I said I would bring him Cynthia, alive and unharmed. He said, quote, 'And if you don't, Harvey, you will wish you had never been born.' That may sound like a bit of nasty rhetoric if you don't know Smedly. Do you know what he is capable of?"

"I know that this cab driver is capable of murdering us, and he's going to, Harvey."

I have to admit that he was an excellent driver, or perhaps

only a lunatic. While I had been talking, he crossed the parkway, and now he was screaming through a Queens suburban street at sixty miles an hour, the olive-green Dodge carrying Kelly trying desperately to hang onto his tail. My heart went out to our driver, who had no idea that a cop was chasing him and that if he were caught, he would do ninety days at best and maybe a hundred dollars more; and I felt it was my duty to offer him another five.

"Jack, goodby to them," he chortled, took a curve on two wheels, raced into a cemetary, twisted and turned along a mile of cemetery road with which he was apparently familiar, came out on another suburban street, screamed along, doubled, doubled again, and then somehow shot into the parkway with the skyline of Manhattan in front of us. It was beautiful, and of Kelly, there was neither sign nor smell.

"You're very free with your money when you're buying mayhem," Lucille said. "We could have had dinner in the Plaza—"

"We made it."

"What?"

"We dumped Kelly."

"If he had taken us to New York, I know thirty-three ways of losing your friend, Kelly, without risking our necks—and this is typical of you and every other American male weaned on television."

"Lady," the driver said, "you got a grudge against affluence?"

"Oh, tend to your driving," Lucille said in despair.

"On driving I don't need lessons, lady. But if I make a buck the hard way, a man must eat."

I said nothing, and in due time we came to the Ritzhampton. "Thank heavens for that," Lucille said.

"For what?"

"We're alive."

"Yeah. Sure." I was thinking about my office, which I had not seen since yesterday morning. If I called Hunter, he would chew my ear off and demand that I put in an appearance immediately; but if I did not call, the whole thing might be off and I would still be out chasing my tail. So I decided to call Mazie Gilman, in research, who always knows all that is going on; and we went into the hotel where I used one of the pay telephones in the lobby. While I was dialing the number, Lucille waited outside the booth, the Donnell Branch forgotten and herself a permanent delinquent. Then Mike Jacoby the house detective came by. Out of a corner of my eye, I saw him fall all over himself when he saw Lucille. I watched him talking to Lucille while Mazie demanded to know where I had been.

"Canada. Yes, you can tell Hunter. I'm hot on the trail. What's happened?"

"Nothing," Mazie said, except that Hunter was swearing all over the place and sore as hell that he could not lay hands on me.

"Tell him he'll hear from me late this afternoon."

"It won't satisfy him."

"Tell him to drop dead," I said.

But it was not as easy as that to get rid of Mazie, and while she was filling me in on every detail of the day, Jacoby and Lucille were chopping away with interesting talk, not a word of which I could hear, and then suddenly Jacoby bowed, kissed Lucille's hand, and sauntered away. I guess I hung up on Mazie. I came out of the booth and asked Lucille, "Did I just see what I saw?"

"What do you think you saw?"

"Did I just see that jerk kiss your hand?"

"Yes, and I think it's very sweet, very continental."

"The closest he ever came to continental is Newark, New Jersey. Where did he go? I want to talk to him."

"He went to get a razor cut. I talked to him."

"A razor cut?"

"It's a special kind of a haircut. It costs three dollars. He gets a regular haircut every two weeks and a razor cut once a month."

"Good. You know his tonsorial habits from A to Z. But I want to talk to him now."

"I did talk to him, Harvey."

"Not your talk. Mine. You know that. I wanted to ask him whether Cynthia and the count came back here. Hell—there are twenty things I wanted to ask him."

"Of course they did—and that shows how clever you are, Harvey. Never would it have occurred to me. But never. They came right back here, just like homing pigeons."

"And?"

"And nothing. They are right here. Upstairs in the bridal suite."

"Now?" I demanded excitedly.

"Now. Of course, Harvey. And isn't that wonderful—all that money you are going to make."

I looked at her strangely. "What's all this about money?"

"Don't you think we work well together, Harvey?"

"I think it's time you stopped being sick and went back to the Donnell Library. When is Jacoby coming back?"

"After his razor cut, he goes to lunch. He asked me to go to lunch with him. He said he would take me to the Colony. He said he'd bet his last nickel that you never took me to the Colony."

"He's a great house detective. He sure is. All right, you can either stay here or go back to work. I'm going up to the bridal suite."

She gripped my arm, looked me square in the eye, and said coldly, "You would do that, Harvey Krim. After I run the whole race with you—you dump me. Only a rat would do that."

"I'm only thinking of you."

"I go with you or I make a scene," she said.

"You wouldn't do that."

"Try me."

"You go with me," I said.

We went to the elevator, where I told the operator, "Seventeenth floor—bridal suite."

"Are you announced?" the elevator operator wanted to know.

"Of course I am announced," I said, and made a note to point out to Lucille afterwards that a calm sense of assurance and imperturbability could pass one in almost anywhere. At the seventeenth floor, there was a small landing with three doors.

"The one in the middle is the Executive Suite," the operator explained. "The one on the right is the Presidential Suite. The one on the left is the Bridal Suite."

"Anyone else been up except the count and his bride?"

"Not for the Bridal Suite. But there's been a lot of strange ones for the Presidential Suite."

"Don't tell me the President's here?"

"He don't stay at this hotel, Jack. What's presidential in there is the price."

His board was flashing, and as much as he might have desired to stay there and gape at Lucille and share my bright wit, he had to get about his business. It surprised me how many people enjoyed watching Lucille.

"Well," I said to her, "here it is. Cynthia come home."

She held my arm for a moment. "Harvey—"

There was a new and different note in her voice, and I looked at her curiously.

"Harvey—it's not right."

"It never is."

"Don't you feel anything? It's not right. You want to hear something—music, voices. I don't hear anything."

"Soundproofing," I said. The little foyer had a rich rug, tapestry-vinyl walls, a bench in the neo-Greek style, and a tiny table that supported a vase of fresh flowers. "Well built, posh."

"How did we get up here so easily?" she wanted to know.

"The elevator."

"Harvey, don't be a nut. Do you have a gun?"

"Are you crazy? What would I do with a gun?"

"You're a private eye, aren't you?" Lucille demanded. "Don't private eyes carry guns?"

"I'm an insurance investigator."

"Harvey, wait for Jacoby."

"That's a laugh. Jacoby—the continental op. That's pretty good, isn't it. You know, continental manner—"

"For heaven's sake, Harvey, don't spell out your silly puns. All I want to know is why we can't get Sergeant Kelly or that man Rothschild. What are cops for? Do you know, I never saw a film about this kind of thing where all the trouble couldn't have been avoided by calling the police. You know that. The film comes to a point where everyone in the audience with an ounce of intelligence is muttering, Call the cops, call the cops. But no. The idiot hero that someone in Hollywood dreamed up knows better. He doesn't have to call the cops. He goes on himself, and then wham—!"

"I told you to wait downstairs," I whispered angrily.

[125]

"OK, Harvey."

There was an ornamental brass knocker on the door. It sounded three clear notes when I used it. The door opened. I entered. Lucille entered behind me, and then the door closed behind both of us. A tall, sunburned man stood alongside the door. He was at least six-foot-two. He wore a gray suit with very narrow trousers, embossed cowboy boots with silver inlay, and a broad-brimmed cowboy hat. In his hand, he held a forty-five caliber automatic pistol, fitted with a silencer. He smiled at us without parting his lips, nodded, and motioned us into the living room with his gun. Perhaps you have never considered how expressive a small motion with a gun can be; let me assure you that it is a complete essay, detailing all the history of the motioner's relationship to guns. This one had a long and intimate relationship, and it gave me no desire to test the accuracy of my guess. I went into the living room and Lucille followed me.

In the living room was the object—or objects—of my search. A tall, well-made young lady was sitting in a chair—in a sort of semi-catatonic state. A body lay stretched out on the floor, and it did not require a second look to realize that this was Count Gambion de Fonti, né Valento Corsica. He had been a neatly-groomed and not uncomely young man, and he wore a white carnation in his lapel, which made him look rather like a toppled department store dummy. Except that dummies do not bleed, and he had bled rather profusely from three bullet holes in his chest.

And sitting here and there around the room were four other men, one of them incredibly obese. The name popped back into my mind from somewhere, "Fats Coventry." It was an odd name. Then I remembered what Rothschild had said.

Chapter 11

The fat man pointed to an unoccupied loveseat. "Sit down, folks," he drawled. "Make yourselves easy and comfortable. Don't be strange. This here is just a friendly little gathering."

We sat on the loveseat. Cynthia came out of her catatonic state to look at us, and I said, "You're Cynthia Brandon, right?"

She began to bawl. One of Lucille's hands found mine, and she whispered, "Harvey, I'm scared."

"Now, now, honeychild," the fat man said, "you're among gentlemen. Southern gentlemen. No reason to be alarmed."

The three men who had been sitting down when we entered rose now, and at a nod from the fat man, approached me.

"Frisk him," the fat man said.

"I don't carry a gun."

They went over me quickly and expertly.

"Lady's purse," the fat man said.

They went through Lucille's purse.

"Clean," said the very tall, tight-lipped smiler who had ushered us in.

They were all dressed alike—gray flannels, Texas style, narrow trousers, padded shoulders and quilting on the pockets of the jackets. Their expensive pearl-gray hats were parked here and there around the room, and they all wore cowboy boots and string ties and diamond pinky rings. Except for one who was very young and quite short, they were all oversized, all lean, all in their late thirties or early forties.

"Myself, I'm Fats Coventry," the fat man said, "and you may have heard of me somewhere in the pasture, Brother Krim—"

"How do you know my name?"

"I believe in knowing what I must know, Brother. Let me introduce the boys. The gentleman who admitted you is Joey Earp, the Descendent. No real relationship to the Earps, but some wit dubbed him the Descendent and it stuck. Feller over there is Jack Selby, whom we call Ringo, and next to him, that pale feller, he's Freddy Upson, the Ghost. Little feller's Billy the Kid. That's all—Billy the Kid. But don't allow size or demeanor to confuse you, Brother Krim—no, sir. How many men you killed, Billy?"

"Nineteen."

"How old are you, Billy?"

"Nineteen."

"When you going to be twenty, Billy?"

"Tomorrow."

"Going to make a mark for every year of your life, Billy?"

"Sure enough."

"How'd you make nineteen, Billy?"

"Gunned that there foreign son-of-a-bitch stretched out on the floor."

Cynthia wailed.

"Shut up, honeychild," said the fat man. "How you reckon to make a score of twenty, Billy?"

"Reckon to gun down that creep sitting there on the sofa, but I can't rightly do so until tomorrow. Don't that make sense, Mr. Coventry?"

"Sure does. You're a good boy, Billy."

"How can you just let him lie there like that?" Cynthia cried out suddenly. "How can you sit here and talk and let him lie there like that?"

"That's a thought," Coventry admitted. "Couple of you boys take him out to the kitchen and put him in a closet or cupboard or something there." Earp and Upson lifted the count, hands and feet, and marched him out of the room.

Lucille took a deep breath, let go of my hand, and said to the fat man, "You are the most extraordinary person, Mr. Coventry, if I do say so. You're totally amoral, aren't you?"

"Just what kind of brand you trying to put on me, Missy?" he asked good-naturedly.

"Don't call me Missy! Don't you dare!"

At that point, I put in a silly TV line, and as frightened as I was, I was still somewhat mortified at saying, "You don't think you are going to get away with this, do you?" Lucille looked at me in amazement. "Oh, hell," I said with disgust. "This is New York City. This is the Ritzhampton Hotel. This is Madison Avenue. What kind of nuts are you?"

The fat man nodded good-naturedly. "You're a maverick, sure enough, Sonny," he said. "You know, I own this hotel."

"What do you mean, you own it?"

"Bought it two months ago for seven million dollars. How about that, Big Joey?" he said to Earp. "Is it the gospel truth or is it not?"

[129]

"Gospel truth," Earp replied.

"And Jacoby? You know Jacoby—the house dick?"

I nodded dumbly.

"He works for me. Amiable boy, but not much between the ears. I'm his boss. That's why he's so amiable."

"You know," Lucille said now, "you don't have to kill us. We didn't see you kill the count."

"Count? Lord, lady, he ain't no count. He's the head of an organization they call the Mafia. You ever heard of the Mafia, Missy?"

Lucille looked at me. I looked at her. "Oh, heavens to Betsy, I am scared, Harvey," Lucille whispered to me out of the side of her mouth.

Fats Coventry grinned and said to "alias Ringo", "Dry, Ringo. How about you get into the kitchen and fetch me a bottle of diet-Pepsi." Ringo hotfooted it into the kitchen and Coventry explained to me, "Watching my weight these days. I never used to before, but I reckon it's time I thought about some of these new-fangled things like cholestorol." The Pepsi returned in Ringo's hand, in the bottle and without unnecessary elegance. Coventry tilted the bottle back and drained it in one long, gurgling swallow. Then he put the bottle aside delicately, patted his stomach and observed that there was something mighty American and homelike in a soft drink. "It's as natural as apple pie," he said. "I don't allow no hard liquor on the roundup or when the hands are working 'round the corral. No, sir. Work and liquor don't mix. Soft drink's different. A hand wants a soft drink to quench his thirst, he's entitled—don't you reckon so, Harvey?"

Now it was "Harvey." I nodded and watched him thoughtfully. His cowboy talk was strictly Hollywood cowboy talk; his performance was strictly a performance; but his "hired

[130]

hands" were real enough, and the guns they carried were no frontier Colts but modern automatic pistols equipped with the best and most effective silencers. His "hands," as he called them, were apparently disciplined and efficient; and all in all, he added up to more than a Texas hoodlum on the bigtown make. I tried to recall some facts about the Coventry gang, and all that I could remember was the name. Texas was out of my territory and such has been the mushrooming of the Dallas insurance companies that New York concerns are not picking up as much business in Texas as they might.

"Tell your little lady that we ain't going to execute the two of you—leastways not tomorrow. Billy the Kid looks to being twenty years old over the next twelve months, and that's plenty of time to put a notch or two in his gun."

"Harvey?" Lucille whispered.

"I think so," I said. "I imagine he's telling us the truth, kid. Just take it easy."

"I like you, I do, Harvey," Coventry said. "Sure enough."

"How do you know my name?"

"Hell to sundown, Harvey, that's like ABC. You sure enough forgot that Jacoby, the house dick, works for me. No. No, he don't know who I am. He's a nice, honest young feller. But I know a good deal about you. I just happen to know that you're the smartest insurance dick in New York City and that the little lady here is Lucille Dempsey and that she graduated this here Radcliffe College up in Harvard Yard or wherever the hell it is and that now she works in the New York Public Library—all of this here information out of Jacoby, who's downright crazy about the girl."

"What else do you know?" I asked him.

"You'd be surprised, Harvey. I happen to know that foreign feller we got stuffed away—where'd you put him, boys?"

[131]

"Laundry bin," Joey Earp replied.

"Good enough. Well, I just happen to know that little feller's one Valento Corsica by name, alias Count Gambion de Fonti, and the new top man in the Mafia—"

A high-pitched wail from Cynthia interrupted this; then the wail was cut off. Suddenly, quite normally, Cynthia said, "He wasn't, of course." She then took several deep breaths.

"Wasn't what, honey?" Lucille asked.

"The head of the Mafia. He really was a count. They paid him ten thousand dollars to do this, and now you've killed him—you're such hateful animals—and I never liked Texas and anyway my father was born there—"

"Come on now, baby," Coventry said soothingly, "don't get all riled over nothing. Texas ain't to blame at all. It's just that this here Mafia been running hog wild for too long, and it's time some citizens saddled up for a posse. We simply got to let them Mafia folks know that their day is done. This here's the first step."

"You mean that's why you're in New York?" I asked him.

"Lord, no, Harvey. We got various and sundry interests in New York, but when the Mafia began putting out a feeler here and there to buy this here hotel, I got suspicious. We been having a bit of trouble with the Mafia on and off. They don't know that we own this shack and they like the location. But I bugged every suite in the place. Don't listen to all of them, but Lady Luck turned our way when my listening man heard about them slipping the count here into the country and marrying him off to some fine, clean-cut American girl, and a Texas girl too. You wouldn't say that was exactly a gentlemanly thing to do, would you, Harvey?"

"Certainly not."

"He was more of a gentleman than you'll ever be," Cyn-

[132]

thia put in, dabbing at her eyes with a small lace handkerchief. I was able to take a good look at her now, and I must admit that she was a striking girl, red-headed, pretty in her own way, which was a sort of lanky, long-faced, long-legged way. "He can afford to be nice to you," Cynthia said to me, beginning to sniffle again. "I'm the only one who saw the poor count murdered—by that little rat there—"

Billy the Kid grinned.

"So I'm the one he has to eliminate, so there'll be no witness to the killing, and if you think I've had one damn bit of pleasure out of being a rich man's daughter, you're mistaken, Mr. —?"

"Krim," I told her. "You just call me Harvey, kid."

"You just call me Harvey," Lucille mimicked in a whisper.

"Lord, Missy," the fat man said, "there's no reason for you to be fretful. What about the eighteen other contracts Billy here done? Might as well be hanged for a cow as a sheep—don't you agree, Sonny?" he asked Billy.

Billy grinned again. He was examining the upholstery of the chair and picking away at it with his fingernail. "You know, Mr. Coventry," he said, "I like this here chair mighty fine. You wouldn't think of shipping it back down to Texas for me, would you?"

"I might just at that, Billy."

He grinned and the other men grinned. It was plain that they were mighty fond of their talented youngster.

"You know what else I'd like to do, Mr. Coventry?"

"Just what, Billy?"

"Why I'd like just to curl up in this here big chair and bang the hell out of that long-legged red-headed girl there."

"Well, maybe that too can be arranged, Billy."

"Over my dead body," Cynthia said.

[133]

"We'll see. Here I've gone and told you that we have no intentions of eliminating you, and right off the mark, you get fresh. I don't like fresh kids. You take a tip from Billy, here. He's mighty respectful. All the time."

"Well, sir, Mr. Coventry," I said, taking a tip, "I can't tell you how relieved I am that you look at the whole matter so philosophically. Since you know all about me, there's no use trying to deceive you. I have only one purpose in mind—to bring Cynthia Brandon back home safe and sound and in one piece."

"I reckoned that was what you had in mind, Harvey. The kid's heavily insured, huh?"

"Well, so, so," I shrugged. "But you know the way insurance companies are, Mr. Coventry. Can't stand to pay out a dollar if there's some other way around."

"I certainly do, Harvey. Matter of fact, I got a piece of a little insurance company down in Dallas. But, do you know, Harvey, you got to make more sense. You wouldn't suggest that I simply let the three of you walk out of here right now?"

"That's what I had in mind."

"Harvey!"

"Well, I mean we could sort of give you our word—"

"Harvey!"

"Well, Goddamn it, what are you going to do with us?"

The fat man thought about that for a while, and then he said, "First things first, Harvey. One hand wipes the other. You got your interests in mind, I got mine. You help me, I help you. You want Cynthia. Well, I want a little something too, matter of fact. Yes, sir."

"You got a proposition—make it."

Both girls looked at me now, and I wondered what each

was thinking, and I got no clue. Lucille's eyes moved from me to Coventry and then back again to me and then around the room over that curious circle of Texas hoodlums. Cynthia watched only me. I watched Coventry and then I watched Billy the Kid, who curled in his chair like a big cat, the gun in his shoulder holster bulking under his arm.

"Trade even, Harvey," the fat man said. "Now I sure as hell can't turn you loose here in New York with Valento Corsica stuffed into the laundry bin, can I?"

I shrugged, and Cynthia snapped, "He was not Valento Corsica."

"So I got to get the body to the bottom of the river, maybe, and then get someone else to take title to this here hotel, and then finish up my business and get out of New York, and that's a heap of trouble you and these girls caused me, Harvey, so what makes sense is for me to kill the lot of you and put you on the bottom of the river with Count Gambion, don't it?"

"But you got a proposition."

"Indeed I have, Harvey. I'm ready to trade even—what I want, for the girls. Well, now, I might have to take you all down to Texas with me and give you a week or two at the ranch until the heat is off, but that's the kind of fine healthy vacation you city folks really never get to have."

"And what do you want?"

"Not money, Harvey—because even if I kidnapped that there kid, it would only be for peanuts. Anyway, kidnapping's a sucker's game. I want some real goods, and I think you're the boy can lead me to it."

"Oh?"

"Yes, sir. You heard of something called *Aristotle Contemplating the Bust of Homer?*"

"What?"

The four hired hands grinned with pleasure.

"Yes, sir, Harvey—*Aristotle Contemplating the Bust of Homer.*"

"He means the painting, Harvey," Lucille explained icily. I did not need her explanation; I was a step ahead of her and with the fat man.

"It's in the Metropolitan Museum of Art, Harvey," Lucille said. "They paid two million dollars for it."

"That's right, Harvey," said the fat man. "You got a mighty smart-ass little girl there. That's right where it is—in the Metropolitan Museum of Art. And I hear your company carries the coverage on that building."

"Come off it, Mr. Coventry," I said. "No company in the world is big enough to insure the Met. We carry some of the coverage—so do ten other companies, and then it's reinsured and laid off and reinsured again, because you couldn't find an adding machine large enough to add up the dollars and cents worth of what's in that building up there on Fifth Avenue."

"I know that, Harvey." Coventry smiled. "But what matters to me is not how much coverage you got there, but the fact that you got entry, Harvey—entry, and that you know how their protection works. I don't reckon I want the whole building, Harvey—I just want that one little old painting, because I got me a client down in Texas who is ready to put five million dollars on the line when I turn it over to him. And five million dollars, tax free, Harvey, is nothing to sneeze at. No, indeed, Harvey—not at all."

Chapter 12

If there is any generalization that fits fat men, it is an awareness of a human being's need for nourishment, and Coventry had a very substantial lunch sent up for us, champagne and four kinds of sandwiches and salad and cheese and fresh fruit, red wine for those whose taste it matched, coffee, a tray of pastry, mints and a bottle of brandy. It was a magnificent table, wheeled into the Bridal Suite by Billy the Kid. When I asked him to help himself, he shook his head. "I don't eat with the guests," he said. "I'm just a hand." It was very humble and straightforward of him. They had left us alone there. When I went out the back service door, there was Jack Selby alias Ringo, picking his teeth. When I poked my head out of the front door, there was Billy the Kid, practicing his draw from a shoulder holster. "But you just caint draw quick with one of these here automatic pistols. Give me a silencer any day of the week. What kind of gun do you hanker after, Mr. Krim?"

"Wrigley's Spearmint," I said, making a lousy pun out of it, and I slammed the door and tried the telephone. The telephone was dead, which I might have expected.

Lucille was pouring champagne and trying to get Cynthia to accept a plate of sandwiches, and paused just long enough to suggest that I get right onto the phone and call the police.

"Good thinking," I agreed.

"Now do you think I'm going to eat sandwiches with poor Gambion stuffed into the laundry bin? What kind of a heartless thing do you imagine me to be? You're as bad as my mother."

"Gambion's not in the laundry bin any longer," I informed her. "They wrapped him up in spare sheets and sent him down the laundry chute. He's probably snug at the bottom of the river right now."

"What a rotten, callous thing to say!"

"I'm only trying to help your appetite. Myself, I am starved." I took a sandwich, downed it in two bites, drained a glass of champagne and followed that with another sandwich. They were delicate sandwiches and hardly more than a bite each.

"How do you know?" Lucille asked me.

"What?"

"About Corsica."

"He's not Corsica," Cynthia exclaimed. "Why don't you listen to me?"

"Coventry told me," I answered Lucille, and then asked Cynthia, "How do you know he's not Valento Corsica?"

"Oh, because the poor jerk broke down and told me. He's the penniless younger son of a penniless count, and he lost his nerve and we never got married but he went through with the motions. He was a sweet little guy and he was gay, but that wasn't his fault but the bombshell he had for a mother, and they gave him the money he needed so desperately to go through the computer dating routine and lay a phony trail to

[138]

snarl up immigration and the fuzz, and I liked the poor little shnook, and then, bango. Just like that."

"Eat something. You'll feel better," Lucille said.

She started on the champagne, downed two glasses as if it were water, and then began to eat. For a skinny kid, she had a healthy appetite, and the sandwiches just kept going down. She explained to Lucille that her ability to talk with a mouth full of food stemmed from her private school training.

"It's one of the few advantages of being a rich kid. Can you imagine, putting him down the laundry chute!"

"Well, you don't play footsie with the Mafia. He should have thought twice."

"You still don't believe me."

"Maybe, maybe not. Who knows?" I thought about it for a moment. "It doesn't matter. Whoever he was, he took their cash. What followed, followed."

"Come on, Harvey," Lucille said, "don't turn moralist. You're going to cooperate, aren't you? I mean his lunatic scheme to rob the Met."

"Yes," I said. "I am."

"Oh, great—just great."

"Look," I said, "isn't it about time both of you ninnies got some sense into your heads. I don't cooperate—he kills the three of us. I help him pull it off, he's grateful—we got a chance. That's how it works—just that way."

I took my notation pad out of my pocket and wrote down, "The whole place is bugged, stupid." I showed it to both of them, and then I wrote, "We play it by ear, do you understand?" Then I went into the john, tore up my notes and flushed them down the toilet. When I returned, Cynthia was observing me with a speculative glint in her eyes.

"He's thirty-six years old," Lucille observed coldly. "That

[139]

makes him sixteen years older than you, lovey, unless you have the popsie complex that's rampant today. Furthermore, he's divorced, unreliable, neurotic and poor. He has a reputation for being smart, but now that he's a working part of a plan to rob the Metropolitan Museum of Art, I have my doubts about that too."

"I think he's adorable," Cynthia said.

At that moment, the doorbell rang, and I rushed to swing the door open with some delirious hope that I would see the ulcer-drawn face of Lieutenant Rothschild. Fats Coventry stood there.

"The girls will be safe enough, Harvey," he said. "They have a twenty-one inch color television, and I am having newspapers and magazines sent up, so I reckon they'll be able to pass the time smartly. You come along with us, and help us chew over some of our smoke signals—"

Under the Hollywood cowboy talk, I seemed to detect a trace of Brooklyn or perhaps Patterson, New Jersey, but well-hidden. He had astonishingly small feet and he minced in his cowboy boots and he tugged at the fringes of my memory. We went out of the Bridal Suite into the small landing and then into the Presidential Suite—which was pretty impressive, I imagine, even to Presidents. It was all done like a studio set for a film about Dolly Madison and how the British burned Washington, D.C., full of curved table legs, gilded mirrors acting as eagle perches and fake antique Aubusson carpets of pale blue, with gold and ivory trim.

Coventry had the pride of a true host as he exhibited the wonders of the place, although he had to admit that as yet no President had tried the bed. "Now you would think, wouldn't you, Harvey," he complained, "that a Texas President would maybe throw a little business our way. No, sir.

He goes straight back to the Carlyle, like there wasn't no other hotel in the city."

The smoke signals were being chewed over in the study, where black leather set the keynote and busts of the first President and the Great Emancipator faced each other sternly. The cowhands sat around in their shirtsleeves—that is, Freddy Upson and Joey Earp did, while the other two did guard duty—with their forty-five automatics strapped visibly in their armpits and with long panatellas to sweeten the taste of their Bourbon. I was served with the same ingredients, and then Coventry called the meeting to order with a simple, straight forward question:

"How about it, Harvey—can the Met be robbed?"

"Any place can be robbed if you put enough brains and muscle into it. The burglar-proof box is a myth. Whatever one man makes, another man can break into."

"I like that kind of an answer," Coventry said. "Yes, sir— yes, indeed. That's a sensible answer and what I would expect from a man in your profession, Harvey. What's the catch?"

"Do you think you could get into the Met after closing?" I demanded. "You must have looked it over."

Coventry nodded at Upson. "Freddy there's done more burglar jobs than you could shake a stick at, Harvey. He looked it over. Tell him what you think, Freddy."

Upson stretched his legs and drawled, "A kid could break into that place, I reckon."

"How?"

"The way I figure it, the easiest spot is the ground floor, where they have that there Junior Museum, as they call it. You know the spot?"

I nodded.

"Well, they got a door leading from the parking lot, a

[141]

double door, two sets, and just strong enough to be opened with a pair of scissors. The outside set is glass, one inch thick. Cylinder lock at the base of each door. I got keys to open the lock and if I didn't have keys, I could open it with a slide-hook, or I could use a set of double-action clamps to pluck it clean. Any one of the three ways would take all of thirty seconds. The inside door is wood, two inches thick, same type locks at the bottom of each door. Both sets are swinging doors meeting at center without a jamb. Everything goes right, I can go through both doors in ninety seconds; I get a bad break, it takes me two minutes. Then I'm in a sort of medium long hall where they got models of these here old ranch houses, places called the Parthenon and such—you know, them places where the old gods spent their time. You go through there, up a flight of stairs, turn left and into the big main entrance way. Then up the big stairs into the Italian room, turn right, third room turn left, and there you are with this here painting there on the wall and not one cotton picking reason not to take it down and whistle off with it."

"How about that, Harvey?" Coventry asked.

"Like he said, getting in is no problem."

"Right, Harvey. But getting out?"

"There's the rub," I said. "Getting out. You just wouldn't get out."

"Unless you got us out, Harvey."

"Impossible. Good heavens, do you know what happens when you open the first lock?"

"That's just what we need you for, Harvey," the fat man said with satisfaction. "What happens?"

"It breaks a circuit. That's basically the difference between the Metropolitan Museum of Art and say, for example, the Museum of Natural History. It underlies the difference in the insurance rates they pay. Not that there isn't great wealth

[142]

in the Natural History building but most of it is not market-
able, and their whole outlook is different. That's how those
young hoodlums from Florida managed to get in and walk off
with the jewels. No one thinks of Natural History and jewels
together—not even the curators. But here, one small exhibition case can and often does hold over five million dollars
worth of value, and the point of view is different. You don't
rob Fort Knox. You don't rob the Met. That's just about
what it amounts to. Every single entry, door, window, air-
shaft, chute, sewer or crawlspace has some sort of mechanism
for electronic response. There it is."

Coventry smiled. "All right, Harvey—we open the outside
doors. We break a circuit. What happens?"

"Well, to begin with, there's a location board in the central security office."

"In the Museum?"

"That's right. In the Museum basement—or the ground
floor, as they call it. A tiny light pinpoints the point of dis-
turbance, and at that moment, the guard on duty knows only
that the circuit has been broken at a certain point. When you
open the second set of doors, he can conclude that a deliberate entry has been made. But even before then, he has picked
up the night guard in the Junior Museum wing on walkie-
talkie and directs him to investigate. There would be a night
guard in the Special Exhibition Galleries—that's the front,
downtown wing of the building, and nights he would cover
Greek and Etruscan as well—and he'd pick up on the walkie-
talkie and cover the stairs, also going down once the night
guard in the central nave had joined him. By now, they know
it is deliberate entry, so they have their guns drawn, and
while your Texas hands are pretty good, they're pretty good
too."

"A sort of range war—right, Harvey?"

[143]

"Right," I agreed. "But that is only the internal situation relating to the guards in the area. The captain of the night guards has meanwhile put a general alarm on the city system and is probably on the phone to the Nineteenth Precinct. He can also switch on the Fifth Avenue floodlights—and if it's after midnight, any passing prowl car will investigate. He can open the internal lighting to full, and he can activate alarm bells. But even if he does nothing at all, the broken circuits would signal the Nineteenth Precinct and the Pinkerton office. I sort of think they use the Pinkertons—maybe Holmes."

"By golly, Harvey, that is an arrangement, ain't it?"

"It certainly is, and it doesn't end there. Somewhere in the room with the models of the buildings of antiquity, there's an electronic eye. You trigger that and signal your direction. An automatic camera photographs you, and if it misses you there, it will grab you at one of six points up to the Rembrandt Room. You also detail your route on the location board. But all that is window-dressing, because before you ever get to the Rembrandt Room, you will either be dead or in a range war, as you call it, and if you're not dead, there are already fifty cops around the building and more coming in by the minute —and, well there it is. You just don't pull a heist at the Metropolitan Museum of Art."

"But that's sure enough what we intend to do, Harvey, because either we take that painting back to Texas or you and them two little cuties are going to be staked out and just as dead as dead can be. And you don't think I'm fooling about that, do you, Harvey?"

"No, sir," I answered politely. "I don't think you're fooling about that at all."

"Then, partner," he said, "figure it out. Just like you said before, Harvey—there never was no place couldn't be robbed,

[144]

you put enough muscle and brains into it. Well, sure as hell, you ain't got the muscle. Let's see about the brains."

I sat there and looked from face to face, and the faces of the ranch hands returned my look with interest and respect. I had laid out a most impressive and intricate picture of how the Metropolitan Museum of Art protected its treasures, but it was an invention from the word go; and the truth of it was that I had no more notion of the Museum's protective system than these cowboy baboons who faced me. Maybe the Museum indulged in some of the gambits I had mentioned, maybe not. But since these men of the world—southwestern style—believed the Rube Goldberg contraption I had spelled out for them, it might just be that someone else was damn fool enough to build it.

Why they should dream that an insurance investigator would be privy to the protective measures of one of the world's greatest houses of art treasures, I couldn't imagine. Maybe that's the way it is done in Texas, where insurance is almost as big a moneymaker as oil wells, but that is certainly not the way it is done here; and if I could bluff a knowledge of the Museum's floor plan, it was only due to the fact that Lucille Dempsey would drag me there occasionally of a Sunday and the fact that I have a good memory for layout. Where the bluff would get me, I had no idea—except a feeling that it postponed the inevitable; but not for a moment did I believe that the inevitable would be different. Sooner or later, the fat man would kill the three of us; and even the pretense of a different conclusion was a pretty obvious pretense. That was the way the fat man's mind worked, and he knew that I knew it was the way his mind worked. He knew that I would delay it and play along with him as long as possible, hoping for a break—any break, and he also knew that I knew he knew. That was why he knew I would help him steal the picture—

the one thing that he could not manage if he killed me; but what he did not know was that I could no more steal that Rembrandt than I could steal the Pope's Crown. Perhaps he gave me credit for brains. I agreed with him; under any circumstances, I had more sense than he did.

"Because you see, Harvey, there's two things against us, and you are going to figure a way around those two things."

"Oh? Two things? There are forty things—"

"No, sir, Harvey. Two things. Getting into the building and the alarm system. Just them two things."

"All right," I agreed. "I'm with you. The first is easy. We can't get into the building after it closes, and we sure as hell can't do anything about the alarm system until we're in the building. So the answer leaves us no alternative. We have to be in there when it closes and we have to be hidden well enough to remain safely after it closes."

Joey Earp's face lit up with pleasure. Freddy Upson forgot himself and grinned. It was a relief to know that one of the hands could smile.

"He's all right, boss," Joey Earp said. "He's a pretty miserable little squirt, but he's smart."

I just want to put it down here, for the record, that I am five feet and ten inches tall—short perhaps for a Texan—but a height I have always considered respectable enough.

"Maybe," said the fat man. "Where do we hide, Harvey?"

"For that," I replied, "I would want to stroll around the Museum for a bit and work on it."

"Are you some kind of nut, Harvey?" he asked, dropping the cowboy talk completely for the first time. "You don't leave this hotel or our sight until we go out to make our hit on the place."

"No?"

[146]

"No, Harvey."

"Oh. Well, then it's got to take some thinking."

"That's what you're here for, Harvey. You think. Otherwise we don't need you. Otherwise, the laundry chute—like the count."

"I'll think," I agreed.

"Good."

I thought about it for the next ten minutes, while they waited. It was not easy. Try it some time. Take the Museum and figure out a place to hide—a place you can get into and out of without attracting undue attention. It's not easy, and it's got to come up ridiculous—as ridiculous as the rest of it. It had to and it did. After ten minutes, I told him I had it.

"Where, Harvey?"

"Under the beds."

"Don't put me on, Harvey. I don't like that."

"I'm not putting you on," I protested. "Listen to me. Back of the uptown end of the Museum, there's an elbow they call the American Wing. It's full of old rooms from Colonial times, and in these rooms are beds, and under these beds is one of the only spots in the building that a man could hide. Or two men."

"Or six, Harvey?"

"Or six. Six?"

"Just get this straight, Harvey, in case you're playing games with me. You go into that building with Joey Earp and Freddy here, and the two girls go with you. One squeak, one false move, and it's all over for the girls."

"My God," I protested, "that's one sure way to louse it up. You can't pull this off dragging two dames around."

"He's right, boss," Freddy Upson put in. "Any dame's a

[147]

maverick. You ask me, put some tape on their kissers and set them in the car outside."

"I'll think about it," the fat man admitted grudgingly. "Let's talk about that alarm system you spelled out, Harvey."

I invented and contrived desperately. Who knew whether the Museum had a Rube Goldberg alarm system? Probably they had some kind of alarm system or maybe they depended on a night patrol of guards. I didn't even know that.

"Well, Harvey?" the fat man prodded.

"Yes. That's it," I said. "You see, it's like a good many of the old buildings in New York—two kinds of current, AC and DC. DC is the old current. They use it to run their elevators and their ventilating system—"

"Mighty peculiar they don't modernize it and switch to AC," Joey Earp put in. "Down our way—"

I just had to be blessed with someone who knew more about electricity than I did. "As a matter of fact," I said, "they've had modernization plans drawn up for years, but it's got to cost them something over a million dollars and they're too damn chintzy to spend the money." I talked very rapidly. "The important thing is that it comes in over one hundred-amp fuses, same as the alternating current. Every two fuses locked in together gives them the draw on two hundred-amp service, that is the alternating current which feeds the alarm and the lighting system—"

"Say that again, Mr. Krim?" Joey Earp asked, frowning.

"Come to think of it, the alarm system is on the direct current, and it feeds out of a single hundred-amp DC circuit."

"DC?" Joey Earp asked.

"Right. It just happens to be damn lucky that they got the DC there, because this location board, which is a by-product

[148]

of our rocket research, and which was installed last year by Texas Instruments, has to have DC."

"Texas Instruments?" the fat man asked with a show of respect.

"Right."

"You follow all this, Joey?" he asked Earp.

"Sort of. Tell you the truth, Boss, I can wire a house and change a fixture, but this here electronic stuff is way out in the pasture for me. I guess if Harvey says so, that's the way it is."

"The point is," the fat man said, "to know where the fuses are. Do you know that, Harvey?"

I nodded sagely.

"Can you pull them?"

I nodded again.

"That's it. OK, Harvey, I want you to take a few hours, think about it, and set your plans. The Museum closes at five. It's three now. We'll leave in about thirty minutes."

That was great, simply great. I was not wholly sure what a hundred-amp fuse was or looked like—much less its location.

Chapter 13

Back in the Bridal Suite, Cynthia sat at a table bent over a sheet of paper, while Lucille observed her without joy. Billy the Kid played happily with his automatic, standing with legs spread, while he twirled the gun and sighted at imaginary targets here and there in the room.

"Like a happy child," the fat man said when we had come through the door. "That's Billy."

"Afternoon, Mr. Coventry," Billy said politely, covered a spot on the ceiling, pursed his lips and went, "Pow!"

"Will you please tell that cretin to stop!" Lucille snapped.

"*I am fluent in (a) Spanish, (b) German, (c) French, (d) Yiddish, (e) Italian,*" Cynthia said. "If you would only not abuse him, you might find that there is a better side to him, as indeed there is to every human being—" This to Lucille.

"Maybe a little Spanish," Billy the Kid said.

"What on earth is she doing?" I asked Lucille.

"*My race is (1) Caucasian, (2) Negro, (3) Oriental, (4) Eurasian, (5) Kanaka,*" Cynthia said.

"She's giving him a dating test," Lucille explained.

"Pow," went Billy in Lucille's direction. "What in hell's a Caucasian, ma'am?" he asked Cynthia.

[151]

"Where does she find dating tests?"

"You tell that runt," Lucille said to the fat man, "that if he points that gun of his at me again, I am going to break him in two."

"Wouldn't a little kindness pay?" Cynthia demanded.

"Billy's just Billy," Coventry said. "He sure don't mean no harm. He's just full of good clean fun, ain't that the case, Billy?"

"Sure enough."

"As for those computer tests," Lucille said, "she carries them around with her."

"No."

"And I have had enough of this whole thing," Lucille said. "Are you going to rob the Museum for them?"

"That's a peculiar way to put it."

"Well, are you?"

"Yes."

"Harvey, I think you are absolutely out of your mind."

"Yes."

"Did anyone ever tell you, Miss Dempsey," the fat man said, "that you are a damned talkative woman. Don't you ever shut up?"

"Most people consider me (a) introverted, (b) extraverted, (c) moody—"

"Will you stop with that stupid test?" I said to Cynthia. "Goddamn it, don't you have any sense. You're two steps away from being scragged and sent down the laundry chute, like your friend the count, and I'm involved up to my neck in a lunatic robbery, and all you can think about is giving that murderous little bastard a computer test."

Billy the Kid spun around, took two quick steps, and jammed the pistol into my stomach. "Nobody gets away with that."

[152]

"I'm sorry. I apologize."

"I got away with it," Lucille said.

"For God's sake, don't make him angry." I begged her. "He's my friend."

"The hell I am," said Billy the Kid.

"Be his friend, Billy," the fat man said generously. "He's going to lead us in and out. He's one of us. He's how we take the picture. No Harvey, no picture."

"Him?"

"That's right—Harvey."

"I wouldn't trust that noaccount bastard as far as I could throw him."

"That's how far," the fat man said good-naturedly.

"Are you interested in this analysis or are you not?" Cynthia asked Billy the Kid.

"Drop dead," he said to her.

She had spirit, no question about that, and she shed her love in two seconds flat, leaped to her feet, took two long steps toward Billy the Kid and let him have a good, solid one in the direction of his face. But like so many women, she telegraphed her slap, and he dodged it, grabbed her arm and twisted.

"Let go of her, you crumby little bastard!" I shouted.

He let go of her and put his gun in my stomach again. "Ah got to kill him," he pleaded with the fat man. "Ah got to."

I entered my counter plea with much more desperation, pointing out to Coventry that if I went, so did his hopes to lay his pudgy hands on the Rembrandt. "Am I or am I not a member of your outfit? And furthermore, his finger's shaking. Please—all I am asking is to get that gun out of my stomach."

"Put the gun away, sonny," Coventry said. "Work first—then fun."

[153]

Lucille allowed him to put the gun back into his shoulder holster this time before she said, "Oh, yes, indeed—work first and then fun. Harvey, have you lost your senses? Do you think they're going to let you get away after this, Harvey? Do you think they're going to trust us and allow Cynthia and me to walk away from all this. They are not!"

"Women are mistrustful critters," Coventry observed. "Madam, be sensible. Harvey is one of us. To inform on us is to inform on himself—and I reckon that's the last thing he has on his mind."

It was—but only because too many other things preceded it, namely: (a) Even if by some miracle I managed to survive in this gang of Texas lunatics, the chances of the girls surviving were absolutely nil. (b) My own survival would be a miracle indeed, for I couldn't even remember properly whether there was a bed in the American Wing of the Museum, much less one that could be crawled under. (c) I had no notion of where a fuse box might be, and less notion of what to do with one if I located it. (d) The whole scheme of stealing the Rembrandt was an idiocy.

Those were only a few of the details that would precede any inclination on my part to inform on them. I could also add Lieutenant Rothschild's reaction when he discovered my own part in the imbecilic transaction. But I suppose that what disturbed me most was a fairly firm belief on my part—and born out of a good deal of experience—that most crooks were nutty as hell and that the reason so many of their schemes worked was that the normal mind—even the normal police mind—was utterly incapable of following or anticipating their reasoning. I had the strange feeling that this might just possibly work.

Chapter 14

As the fat man outlined his plans to me, I experienced more and more acutely a sinking feeling that they might succeed. I supposed that during the course of my life in New York, I have been in and out of the Metropolitan Museum of Art thirty or forty times. Who counts and who attempts to remember? Try it. Where is the Bache Collection? Where is English eighteenth Century? Where is Ingres and Goya and David? However well you know the Museum, just try to map it out in your mind and come up with any sane picture of that enormous warren. Are the American paintings on the way to the American Wing, or do you go by the Art of India? I made a few guesses, which might or might not be right; but at the same time I could recollect no noticeable measures that the Museum took to protect its property. Of course they must take measures, but all I could recollect was an impression of a sleepy, uniformed guard standing here or there.

Suppose they took no measures, I asked myself? Suppose it just worked out the way the fat man planned it, and there I was with two million dollars worth of Rembrandt that I had maneuvered to steal? There was nothing in Coventry's plan that was actually impossible, and its virtue was that it possessed the simplicity that only an idiot could contrive. It would work like this:

Coventry with Ringo and Billy the Kid would be outside. They would have a seven-passenger limousine, one of the enormous special-order cars that you see around town and look like yachts on wheels. In the car, they would have the girls, appropriately gagged and bound. In this, they would drive up to the 81st Street entrance to the Museum at the appropriate time to pick us up with the painting—us being Freddy Upson, Joey Earp and myself. I didn't have enough sense to let them break into the Museum; I had to invent a razzle-dazzle of knowledge that proved it was impossible, and thereby forego the chance of having them caught in the act then and there. Instead, the three of us would be in the American Wing, hiding under a bed, until seven o'clock.

At seven, we would emerge from under the bed. I would extract fuses from somewhere, and then we would walk over to the Rembrandt Room, eliminating any guards that stood in our way, either with pacifiers or silencers, take down the picture, carry it to the 81st Street entrance, exit with it, step into the limousine—which would be somewhat crowded by now but not too much so—and take off for the Bronx. In the Bronx, on East 171st Street, there was a garage Coventry owned and in the garage a trailer truck. The picture would be deposited in the trailer truck along with other merchandise and begin its journey to Texas. On our own next moves, the fat man was understandably vague; and at that point I would not have written insurance on us—that is, the girls and myself—if the premium was even ninety per cent of the payout.

[156]

Such was the plan. Whether it worked or not, our own chances of survival were reduced to practically nothing.

All of this and a good deal more went through my mind as I was driven to the Museum with those two pioneers of Texas culture, Freddy Upson and Joey Earp. It was now Tuesday afternoon, and this whole thing had started five days before with an unloved rich girl who became enamoured of computer dating. I still had untouched, unused, my own secret weapon, infinitely preferably to forty-five caliber automatics, Berettas, stillettos and other instruments of mahem—namely, eighty-five thousand dollars in traveler's checks; and the possibility of using them now occurred to me. But since Billy the Kid was driving the car which transported us, the fat man next to him, I decided that there was time enough. For the moment, I was in the hands of fate; I had nothing in particular to do except be scared.

Coventry underlined this. "The important thing for you to remember, Harvey, is that you're a sort of prairie flower at this moment."

"That's just how I feel," I assured him.

"I mean, if you make a break for it and Joey and Freddy don't get you, why we sure enough got the girls."

"I'll remember that," I promised him.

"On the other hand, Harvey, you got to keep thinking that you're a sort of wave of the future. That's the Texas way to look at things. This here business of kowtowing to the Mafia is over. The new boss of the Mafia is at the bottom of the Hudson River. This here is a return to native American values, Harvey. You follow me?"

"Yes, sir, Mr. Coventry. I follow you."

"The fat man squirmed around in his seat and studied me. We were almost at the Museum now, turning the corner of

83rd Street to come into the Museum driveway. He studied me thoughtfully for a moment or two and then said, "You look peaked, Harvey—mighty pale around the gills. Your hands are shaking. We don't want your hands shaking, Harvey."

I took hold of my left hand with my right hand and explained that my hands had a tendency to shake a bit when I got excited. "It's just coming in for the kill that does it."

"Just get a grip on yourself, Harvey. Zero hour."

"Right."

"Remember. Seven—you go. It should take no more than fifteen minutes at the most. Seven-fifteen, we're at the 81st Street exit. Out and into the car."

Just like that.

We got out of the limousine, and with Upson and Earp towering on either side of me, we entered the Museum. We tried to look like tourists, and I can't imagine much else that we could have looked like. We had a go at Egyptian art, but my Texas colleagues were not very impressed.

"It's pretty old stuff and mostly not in the best condition," Earp said.

"I know an old Mex who cuts tombstones in El Paso," Freddy Upson recollected.

We turned left and passed through a collection of Japanese armor. From there, we went into the main hall of arms and armor, and though both men had made previous visits to the Museum, this was new to them.

"How about that!" said Joey Earp.

They stared fascinated at the iron figures seated on the dummy horses, and Earp finally asked me, "What are they up to, Harvey?"

"They just go at each other with the big stickers."

[158]

"They are the knights of King Arthur's table, you ignorant bastard," said Freddy Upson, and then we passed on into the American Wing. We paused to examine some cases of long flintlock guns, and then we went on to the rooms. We passed a guard and he observed us without curiosity; and I said to myself that if I were running the Museum, my first act would be to have that guard fired. Anyone who could see two tall, cadaverous cowboys with a catatonic insurance investigator between them and not be curious deserved to be fired.

We passed a room with a bed, and then another. We went upstairs one flight, and there were other rooms with beds.

"What kind of a bed do you like?" I asked them.

"We figure to bow to your preference, Harvey."

One thing you have to admit about Texans—they are polite. I picked a room that was momentarily free from observation—guards or citizens—and I pointed to the bed.

"OK, partner," Earp said.

A moment later, the three of us were crawling under the bed. I was all right, but I could see that the Texans' fancy boots stuck out.

"Your feet are sticking out."

"Oh?"

Upson and Earp pulled up their bony knees, so that I was gripped in a sort of vise.

"That's not very comfortable," I told them.

"It ain't for long, Harvey."

"It stops the circulation."

"Feller like you, Harvey, he can do for a little while without circulation."

Footsteps sounded and we stopped talking, and from my low slit of vision, I saw a guard pass through the room. It was toward closing time already and citizens—as opposed to guards—were scarce. It was also very close under the bed and sort of gamey. The Texans were well groomed but there was a healthy stable smell to them—maybe out of using the same boots for walking and riding, or maybe out of my imagination. I have been in one or two strange situations during my life, but nothing as bizarre as hiding under an eighteenth-century bed in the Metropolitan Museum of Art with two bony Texans whose combined IQ could not have been much more than one hundred and fifty. It was a very philosophical situation, and I tried to take it philosophically and even to make a little bit of whispered conversation in the forlorn hope that it might attract the attention of a guard with good hearing, and even more forlorn hope that said guard might get the drop on my two idiot counterparts of Wyatt Earp and Wild Bill Hickcock. I observed that the situation was a little uncommon.

"That's the way the brand falls, Harvey."

"You mean, that's the way the cookie crumbles."

"Ah mean that's the way the brand falls, Harvey, and you just better not raise your voice or me and Joey here, we'll break a rib or two, and that would pain me, that would."

"It would pain me worse," I whispered hoarsely. "But this is a bit outside of the regular line of work of you boys, isn't it? I mean, heisting art?"

"We specialize in banks," said Joey Earp, "but we can turn our hand to most anything. Right, Freddy?"

"Right," Freddy agreed.

Both had their faces up against mine and both could have used a good mouthwash. Cowboys run very strong in cigarette advertisements, but you never hear about a cowboy needing a mouthwash.

"All right," I whispered, "suppose you take the Rembrandt. Who buys it from you?"

"You don't reckon Coventry takes unless he's got a taker?"

"I don't know."

Footsteps again. We held our silence and I breathed their breath. The footsteps passed.

"Who?" I hissed.

"Who?"

"He wants to know who."

"Tell him who," said Freddy.

"Tell him?"

"Oh, what the hell difference does it make?"

They weren't bright. It made no difference because I wasn't going anywhere—probably no further than the 81st Street exit to the Museum. I pulled the fuses. They took the painting. Then goodby to Harvey—and goodby to anyone else who got in their way.

"All right, Harvey. You're a right fine lad. Coventry's going to sell that there painting to Mr. Elmer Cantwell Brandon—just old E.C. Brandon who came up here from Dallas and taught you Yankees a thing or two about turning a dollar."

"Who?" I almost forgot to whisper.

"E.C. Brandon."

"You mean the same one whose kid you got back there?"

"Right the first time, Harvey."

"His kid—oh, no, you goofed this."

"Hell, no, Harvey. Mr. Coventry, he don't goof. No, sir."

"But when he finds out you snatched the kid?"

"He don't find out, Harvey."

"You mean—?"

"You talk too Goddamn much, you do," Freddy said to his partner. "You sure as hell talk too much."

"Harvey's one of us," whispered Joey Earp. "He knows

[161]

just the same as the rest of us the little lady's insured. He works for the insurance company."

"You mean Brandon's in this? You mean he knows you got his kid and—"

"Bless you, no, Harvey," Joey Earp interrupted, breathing warmly into my face. "E.C. Brandon don't know one little cotton-picking thing about all this, but don't he stand to collect a pretty penny when his daughter turns up, stiff as a little old board?"

" 'Cause she's insured," Freddy Upson whispered. "Oh, she's insured right up to the hilt, Harvey."

"Don't either of you have any heart?"

"Nope."

"Just kill anyone—like that? In cold blood?"

"Hell, Harvey," Earp protested, "we never killed no one, without we was paid for it. We don't kill for pleasure."

"Anyway, it ain't us gonna do the killing," said Freddy, but Billy the Kid."

"And what about me? And Miss Dempsey?"

"Oh, you two are sure enough going down south with us, Harvey—you can be sure of that. It's just that Cynthia girl's too much trouble for us to know what to do with her but put her away quietly."

I tried to think, but it was too quiet to think; and a moment later I realized that the Museum was closed, and possibly had been closed for a while now. It seems impossible that any place in New York City could be as silent as that. Joey Earp moved his arm, so that he could look at the luminous dial of his watch. A few minutes of silence, and then he looked at it again.

"Time to hit the trail," he said.

They rolled out, one from each side, and then I crawled

out after them. We weren't clean, and whoever cares for the housekeeping at the Museum might make a note about it. As far as I was concerned, I could pass my last couple of minutes on earth dusty as well as clean but the Texans were fussy about their suits and kept patting and dusting and wiping.

"Maybe you wouldn't think so, Harvey," Freddy Upson explained, "but this here suit of mine cost $422 at Neiman-Marcus."

I was praying so hard that a guard would walk into the room that I couldn't even think of some properly clever rejoinder.

"Now you lead us to that fuse box, Harvey," Joey Earp said.

I led them straight through into the main building toward the Art of India. I had only the most primitive of plans—namely, to lead them in a big circle, through Islamic Art and Far Eastern Art, past the French Sculpture, past Etruscan Art into the special exhibition galleries, where, if by now no guard had turned up, I would make a break for it, and try to outrun their bullets and make enough uproar while doing so to set off whatever alarms there were in the place.

Such was my plan, but it never faced the possibility of being put into effect. We had taken no more than ten steps into the main building when Freddy Upson pointed to a green box on the wall and said,

"I got to give you credit, Harvey old hoss—there's your fuse box, sure enough."

Chapter 15

I heard the footsteps of a guard, and we all froze, and with the same invisible gesture of a magician, Joey Earp's gun was in his hand and the muzzle was touching my ear. I stopped breathing, and the steps went away. There was evidently agreement among all the guards in that place to avoid us. No guards, no alarms, no bells. I tried the green box, and it was locked.

"See," I pointed out to them, "no use. It's locked."

"We are burglars," Freddy Upson replied, not without a note of pride, and then he took a little buttonhook sort of thing out of his pocket and he fiddled around the box and the door was open. There were three fat fuses in it. I pulled each of them out and handed them to Freddy Upson for safekeeping. There were also two large switches, both of which I opened. Nothing happened. Nothing happened when I pulled the fuses. Nothing happened when I opened the switches. The dim night lights did not even flicker.

"Well, that cuts the alarm," I said.

"Your voice is a mite shaky, Harvey."

"Well, bless my soul, wouldn't your voice be a mite shaky if you were here with two oversized Texans who were planning to blow your brains out the moment your usefulness to them was over?"

"Now we don't take kindly to that kind of talk, Harvey," Joey Earp said.

"I don't take kindly to dying."

"You keep making such a fuss about dying, Harvey. Don't you fret now. Did I say anything about dying? Did Freddy? Now you just take us to where that old Dutch painting is hanging and we'll get down to the business we're here for."

I nodded glumly and led them on. We turned right, past the twentieth-century American painting, left and then right again, and there we were, in the Rembrandt room, with the noble painting of Aristotle contemplating the bust of Homer square in the center of the wall to the right. Now we walked forward slowly, and the three of us ranged ourselves in front of the painting, standing and staring at it. After a long moment, I played my last card.

"What does the fat man pay you for a job like this?"

"He don't cotton to being called the fat man, Harvey."

"He pays pretty damn good, Harvey."

"I pay pretty good."

"Come on, Harvey," said Joey Earp, "don't be foolish. If we come out of here without that painting, even Texas ain't large enough to hide us."

"I'm thinking about me, not the painting," I said. "To me, I'm worth a lot more."

"That's reasonable, Harvey."

"I could buy out," I said.

"Harvey!"

"Eighty-five thousand dollars for me, Miss Dempsey and Cynthia."

"Harvey!"

"Real money," I said desperately.

There was a *pop* at that moment, a hollow *pop* that was choking with menace. It's a hard sound to describe if you never heard a silencer. Joey Earp, who was looking at me, stopped looking at anything and he collapsed on the floor. Freddy Upson spun around, clawing for his gun, but the second *pop* was quicker. It was a staged trick, an astonishing illusion. At one moment there were two live Texans; the next moment, two dead ones. They lay there on the floor of the Metropolitan Museum of Art, Joey Earp with a hole in his white-on-white pleated shirt that had cost him $42.50 at Neiman-Marcus, and Freddy Upson with a hole between his eyes and his own Neiman-Marcus shirt untouched. Myself, I remained motionless, uncertain as to whether I was alive or dead, and unwilling to make any sudden motion that would precipitate one condition or the other. It seemed to me that I remained in just this position for quite a while, until a voice said, "All right, Harvey. Turn around—slow and steady, because it is better to be standing than slumbering there with those two slobs on the floor. Am I right, Harvey?"

"Right. But I don't carry a gun."

"I know, Harvey. Just turn easy."

I made a picture for myself of a glass of beer standing squarely on the top of my head, and then I turned so carefully that not one drop of the beer spilled—and came face to face with a man of thirty years or so, a well-knit, good-looking, brown-skinned, hard-faced man, dressed meticulously in what was probably a Brooks Brothers' gray flannel suit and holding in his right hand a Luger pistol fitted with the newest, five-inch German silencer.

"All right, Harvey—right there. Hold it."

[167]

"I don't intend anything personal," I said, "but you seem to know my name—"

"Harvey, they wired the hotel—we wired the hotel."

"They?"

"The shmucks from Texas. Harvey, do I have to draw you a picture?"

"Then Cynthia was right. He was a real count—"

"He was a real count, Harvey. Gambion de Fonti, poor little bastard."

"And you're Valento Corsica."

"Bright, Harvey. The boys said you are stupid. You're not stupid. Maybe a little slow on the pickup, but not stupid, Harvey."

"But no accent—the way you talk, the way you dress—"

"Harvey, the world changes. I spent four years at New York University—School of Commerce, business administration. A year of graduate work at Harvard. The rackets are different, buddy. We don't intimidate—we administrate. And the rough stuff is gone—except at moments."

"And this is a moment?"

"Well, what the hell do you think, Harvey? We hear this fat half-wit from Texas is bent on taking over, so we lay a little intriguing trail with poor Count Gambion. Who ever thought they'd knock over the poor little feller! Well, that's the way it crumbles, but we didn't push it that way. The fat man likes to own hotels, and we would have tied a financial knot around him that he would never unravel. But it didn't go that way, and now I got you on my hands."

"I didn't see a thing," I said firmly.

"Harvey, you simply have no idea how thoroughly we plan a thing. Every loophole plugged, every contingency considered. We even maneuvered the fat man into buying the Ritz-

hampton; we made the loans available to him; we hooked
E.C. Brandon into the deal, and some of us wanted to let it
unfold and then finger Brandon with the picture hidden
away in his cellar. That had virtues, but better to have Brandon outside where we can use him. We got some darling
tapes on him and the fat man and the Rembrandt, and then
we got his daughter."

"You got his daughter? The hell you have! The fat man's
got her, and while we stand here yakking and waiting for the
guards to turn up, he can be putting her away and Lucille
Dempsey with her."

"Don't worry about the guards, Harvey. Don't worry about
the fat man. We got the fat man, Harvey. We got the girls.
We got the two morons he uses for trigger men. You got real
things to worry about."

"Like what?"

"Like being present when I had to kill these two cowboys."

"My God, Mr. Corsica, you saved my life."

"Is that what you're going to say on the witness stand,
Harvey?"

"This won't ever get there. My lips are sealed."

"Don't be a horse's ass," Corsica said.

"No?" I shrugged. "What the hell's the difference—horse's
ass or not. I'm on the short end. The cowboys were leading
me to the last roundup. Now you."

"Don't bracket us, Harvey."

"After all, it was self-defense."

"Harvey," he said patiently, "do you know who I am or
don't you?"

"I know."

"All right," he said. He took a handkerchief out of his
pocket and wiped the butt of the Luger carefully. Then he

[169]

took it by the muzzle and handed it to me. I took it and covered him.

"Don't move," I said.

"Harvey!"

"I'm sorry," I said. "Well, Goddamn it, you give me a gun—"

"Would I give you a loaded gun, Harvey?"

I pointed it at the door and fired. It clicked.

"By golly," I said respectfully, "you went up against them with two bullets—"

"No, Harvey." He took a small Smith & Wesson out of his jacket pocket and covered me. "I got another gun. That makes sense, doesn't it?"

I took out my own handerchief, wiped the butt and dropped the Luger to the floor. It fell with a crash that would have awakened the dead, but our own seclusion was not disturbed.

"There will not be another patrol of guards for thirty minutes or so, Harvey. As for the alarm system, we have disconnected it. So it will do you no good to be petulant."

"Well, I pulled three enormous fuses," I said foolishly. "It's got to do something."

"It did something," he replied patiently. "It cut the current to the converter which changes AC to DC for the old freight elevator. I know the plans and the wring of this place better than the head curator, Harvey. Don't worry. We don't steal art. Shmucks steal art. Texans steal art. We don't. So now pick up the gun, Harvey."

I picked it up. "It's not my gun. Where does it get you?" I asked.

"Let me do it my way, Harvey—yes?"

"Yes," I said.

"The gun is registered in your name, Harvey. The girls will swear that you were taken here under duress and forced to participate in this attempted heist. You will be a hero, Harvey."

"Not in Texas," I said glumly. "Not in the Nineteenth Precinct either," I said, even more glumly.

"Even in Texas, Harvey. The fact of the matter is that Coventry comes from Brooklyn first. They're all wanted in Texas. The fact that you got them both with a gun that had only two cartridges in its magazine—a gun you forgot to load—"

"I'm against violence," I said desperately. I felt sorry for Coventry now. A fat cowboy who comes from Brooklyn is maybe the most pathetic thing on earth.

"You took a life to save a life."

"You're putting me on," I said miserably.

"No, sir, Harvey. I am not."

"Why should you let go of Cynthia?"

"Because a bird in the hand, Harvey, tax-free, is worth a whole flock of birds in the bush."

"What bird in the hand?" I was almost shouting now, and he politely asked me to lower my voice. "What bird in the hand?" I repeated more softly.

"The bird in your pocket, Harvey—the eighty-five grand in traveler's checks that you tried to buy the cowboys with."

"Me have eighty-five thousand? That's a pipe dream. I was conning them. I made that eighty-five out of thin air."

"Harvey," he said coldly, "we tapped your room in Toronto—we got taps all over the hotel—we even got connections in banks. Now, do you give me that eighty-five grand, or do I have to push you around a little and maybe shoot you a little to get it?"

[171]

"You give me both girls?"

"Both."

"When?"

"When you sign the traveler's checks and hand them over."

I reached into my pocket, took out the fat folder of checks, and held it up.

"Sign them, Harvey."

"Where?"

"Sit down on the floor and sign them."

He tossed me a ballpoint pen, and I sat down on the floor, alongside of the two dead Texans, and signed five ten thousand-dollar checks, five five thousand-dollar checks and ten one thousand-dollar checks. Then I pushed the lot over to him.

He picked up the checks, stuffed them into his pocket, and said, "OK, Harvey—stay where you are. Don't move. Count to one hundred, but don't move, because it's been nice and it would be a pity to louse it up at this point. So don't move."

He backed away, and then suddenly he turned around and took off out of the room. I might have gone after him, but it is a lot more likely that I might not have gone after him. In any case, the decision was taken away from me, because before my counting reached twenty, Cynthia and Lucille burst into the room, and Lucille threw her arms around me and kissed me and wept copiously, which was exactly what my battered ego required. Cynthia, on the other hand, stood there forlornly. I expected her to have hysterics, but at that moment Cynthia reached a sort of adulthood.

"I do feel sorry for them," she said, "but they weren't very nice people, were they?"

Chapter 16

"All right, we'll take it from the top again," said Lieutenant Rothschild. "It's only ten minutes past midnight, and Harvey's a strong young feller. It don't matter that I got ulcers and Kelly here's got a wife that's going to divorce him if he don't show up one of these nights. No, sir. None of that matters. We got all the time in the world."

"I told you my story, Lieutenant," I said. I had not only told my story, I had memorized every detail of that office, the yellow walls with their ancient peeling paint, the three old wooden chairs and the two battered tin files, the hundred-watt bulb hanging from the ceiling and the Underwood typewriter circa 1935—and I had even made a feeble and unappreciated crack or two about how the city treats its faithful servants.

"Tell it once more, Harvey."

"Am I under arrest? That's all I want to know. I want to know once and for all whether you intend to arrest me, because if you are going to arrest me, I am damn well going to get a lawyer and see that my rights are protected—"

"Nuts," said the Lieutenant. "That's a load of crap,

[173]

Harvey and you know it. There are any number of things I can do without arresting you, so don't force my hand."

"Such as?"

"Such as killing your license to practice as a private dick. Such as having a chat with the people up there at the company you work for. Such as—"

"All right, Lieutenant. Let's be friends again."

"Just tell it again."

I told it again—interrupted only by one or two unrestrainable guffaws from Kelly. When I finished, I said, "Why don't you explain to that big ape that I'm not doing a comedy routine."

"Because you are, Harvey. Trouble is, you don't listen to yourself. You tell me that you went into the Metropolitan Museum of Art with two of Coventry's cowboys, after you had conned them into believing that you knew how to cut out the alarm system, that the three of you hid under a bed in the American Wing, that you pulled the freight elevator fuses, and then, when you were about to heist the painting, that Valento Corsica appeared, killed the two cowboys with a Luger registered to your name, and then bowed out, leaving the gun with you. How does it sound, Harvey?"

Kelly guffawed again.

"It sounds a little unreasonable," I admitted.

"You know what I say, Lieutenant," Kelly put in. "I say we book him for homicide. He shot two men. That's it. Everything else just clouds the issue. What is clear as day is the fact that he knocked over these two cowboys."

"Sure—that's the one thing as clear as day. The only trouble is that Harvey didn't shoot those two cowboys."

"Why? Because he says so?"

"No." Rothschild shook his head. "You ought to know me better, Kelly. I don't believe what a suspect says even if I can confirm his story with my own eyes. But Harvey here couldn't shoot a rabbit, even if he knew how to shoot, which he doesn't. He never carried a gun and never had a permit for a gun."

"He's got a permit for the Luger."

"So he has. Why don't you give us a straight story on that, Harvey. Just that. Put yourself in my place. I got a murder weapon and I got your fingerprints on it and it's your gun—my God, Harvey, give me a break."

"They registered it in my name. They got the permit," I explained.

"Who?"

"The Mafia."

"Mafia—Mafia—"

"Corsica told me," I began—

"Corsica told you nothing. Corsica is dead. This afternoon they fished his body out of the river. We found the blood-stains on the laundry in the Ritzhampton and we got blood-stains in the laundry chute."

"That's Count Gambion de Fonti. He was not Valento Corsica. He was only a setup, a patsy, a foil for Fats Coventry—"

"Who was shaping up to steal the Rembrandt. I know. You told me. He comes to New York with four cowboy torpedos to steal maybe the most famous picture in the world. For whom? Why? Goddamn it, make some sense!"

He took a deep breath, and then said more softly, "I'm shouting. That could be interpreted as intimidating you. I don't want to intimidate you, Harvey. Why didn't you tell me I was shouting?"

"I don't like to make you angry, Lieutenant," I replied reasonably.

"You don't like to make me angry. You really got a better

[175]

nature or something, Harvey." He turned to Kelly. "Bring up the girl?"

"Which one?"

"The Dempsey girl. With the other one—you tell them kid gloves. She is nobody, only E.C. Brandon's daughter. Here's a couple of bucks. Send out for some more food if she's hungry. What is she doing?"

"She's filling in a form for computer dating."

"What?"

"You know—they run it through a machine and come up with a date."

"Oh? All right—tell the matron to let me know if she gets nervous. If worse comes to worse, we send her home."

"She don't want to go home," Kelly said uncomprehendingly. "They got a sixteen-room flat or something on Park Avenue, but she don't want to go home."

"All right. Send up the other one." He thought about it for a moment. "The kid—well, the hell with what she wants. Give me that two bucks." Kelly handed back the money, and Rothschild said, "Take her home. Send up the Dempsey woman but take the kid home."

"She says no."

"The hell with what she says! Take her home. I want her off my hands."

"It's past midnight—"

"Kelly, take her home!"

Kelly left the room, and Rothschild turned to me and said petulantly, "Look at the kind of hole you put me into, Harvey. Just look at my position. I got enough on you to get an indictment, but you didn't kill those two cowboys. I know that, and yet I can't prove it and neither can you—not with the best Goddamn lawyer in the world. I know you're lying a mile a minute, and so help me God, I would like to hang a

[176]

real big one on you. But this is too big. So you know what I got to do?"

"What?"

"Real wise guy."

"All I said was 'what.' "

"Don't say anything. Because I got to set this up as self-defense. I got to make a hero out of you. Pure self-defense—Harvey Krim, acting in defense of law and order, guns down two deadly Texas killers. You'll be the biggest man in the city tomorrow—and I got to do it. Me."

"Thank you," I said meekly, "but I don't want to take credit for any killings. You know how I feel about violence—"

"You are taking credit, Harvey. One or the other—credit or the rap. Which is it?"

"Credit," I said shortly.

"That's what I like about you, Harvey. Above all, you are a reasonable man."

Lucille was brought into the room at that point by a Detective Banniker. Rothschild told the detective to go and Lucille to sit down. Then he circled his desk and sat down behind it, studying Lucille thoughtfully. Finally, he said, "You're a librarian."

"That's right."

His voice became soft and philosophical, filled with the subtle sadness of lost years never to be regained. He is most dangerous, least to be trusted when his voice does that, but this was something I could hardly convey to Lucille; Rothschild said nostalgically, "Libraries—the whole meaning of my life. You know, radio was just beginning then. We had no television. All our dreams, all our education was in that building—the New York Public Library. It was our Mecca, our oasis, our breath of meaning and hope. Do you know what a librarian meant to me then, Miss Dempsey? To all of us kids?"

Lucille shook her head.

"Civilization!" Rothschild pronounced. 'We lived in a jungle."

"Oh? I feel sorry for you."

"I'm not asking for sympathy. I am trying to evoke a picture—a picture of what the image of a librarian means in my life. A librarian, Miss Dempsey, was something sacred to me."

"I wish Harvey felt that way," Lucille said sadly.

"Him? It would be a miracle if he ever thought of any human being, Miss Dempsey. In those terms, I mean, but don't get me started on Harvey Krim. I have already had a bellyfull of Harvey Krim. The point is, I can't think of a librarian as a liar."

"That's very kind of you, Lieutenant. Only, I imagine librarians will lie when they have to, just as any other group would—"

"Don't disillusion me—please, Miss Dempsey. Just tell me exactly what happened to you tonight."

"But I told it to you already, Lieutenant. I also told it to Sergeant Kelly. I also told it to that nice policeman who took it all down in shorthand—you know, the one who asked me whether I was married. He was very polite. He asked me whether I would ever think about going out with a cop, and I said that I would."

"He's a nice cop," Rothschild agreed. "I'm a nice cop too. I'm a good listener. So tell it again—please, Miss Dempsey."

"Very well," Lucille sighed. "From the airport, we went straight to the Ritzhampton. I talked Harvey into it."

"What! That was my idea!"

"Shut up, Harvey," Rothschild said. "Look, Miss Dempsey, skip that part of it. I want to know what happened after the fat man took Harvey away—Coventry and the two cowboys."

"Well, as I told you, Cynthia cried a good deal. But finally I calmed her enough to play a few hands of rummy. Not that either of us could keep our minds on what we were doing. You just don't quietly play cards when you think you are going to die during the next few hours—"

"Front door and back door locked?"

"Oh, yes."

"Phone dead?"

"Why didn't you smash the windows and throw stuff into the street?"

"Lieutenant, I am not entirely brainless. There's a terrace around that suite. The doors to the terrace were locked. So were the windows. Anyway, there was always a guard outside the doors. So we played cards limply for a while and then I heard that sound I told you about. Outside the front door. A sort of pop. It made me think of a gun being fired but it was not loud."

"Silencer," I said.

"Thanks, Harvey. I never could have figured out that it was a silencer. I needed you for that."

"I also heard the elevator," Lucille said.

"Before?"

"I think so."

"You said you heard it after."

"I think both times. Then I told Cynthia that I was going to try the door again and then maybe start smashing in the windows, just as you said, and maybe get out on the terrace."

"But the door was open."

"Yes."

"And you didn't think it peculiar?"

"I didn't think anything, Lieutenant. I just called out to Cynthia and we both bolted out onto the elevator landing, and I pressed the button as hard as I could—which I don't imagine made one iota of difference, and the elevator came, and the operator didn't appear at all surprised, and he took us down to the lobby, and there was this nice man from Centre Street—that is what you call police headquarters, isn't it?—well he was waiting for us."

"He was not a cop and he was not from downtown," Rothschild said with growing irritation.

"Well, it seems I cannot tell the story to please you, Lieutenant. I do try though. I simply identify this man as he described himself. He said his name was Detective Comaday—John Comaday."

"That's the name of the Police Commissioner, Lucille," I explained gently.

"She knows Goddamn well that it's the name of the Police Commissioner!" Rothschild exclaimed.

"I did not say he was the Police Commissioner, Lieutenant, nor did he. He simply told me that he was a police detective, and he gave me a good Irish name and he had an honest face and a fine pair of frank blue eyes, and Cynthia and I were so happy to see him that we practically fell all over him, and of course I wanted to know how poor Harvey was, and he said that he would take us right to poor Harvey. I was delighted with that. Then he took us through the lobby to the front, and this big Fleetwood was parked there, with a uniformed policeman driving it—"

"Fleetwood! Look around this office, Miss Dempsey! Do

[180]

we look like the kind of an outfit that drives Fleetwoods?"

"I had not yet seen your office, Lieutenant. I do think that if you were to take a scrubbing brush and a paint brush to it, a few hours of work might make it both clean and pleasant."

"I'll keep that in mind," Rothschild said slowly, and then yelled at the door, "Banniker—get me a glass of milk!" He compressed his lips and nodded for Lucille to continue.

"Well, the rest is so simple. I told you the plain, unvarnished truth. They drove us to the Museum. There were three plainclothes policemen at the entrance—the side entrance, you know—"

"They were not policemen," Rothschild muttered.

"I know. But we thought they were, and one of them led us into the Museum and upstairs, and then through another room, and then he pointed, and he said that right there in the next room, Harvey and two right-thinking men were waiting for me. I do think the joke was in poor taste. You don't mock the dead, even if they are killers—don't you agree? Well, we started to go, but he said to hold up just a moment. Then a man came out of that room, a nice-looking man who was grinning, and he nodded, and the other policeman let go of us, and then we ran into the room, and there was Harvey. And the two dead Texans, of course."

"Just like that?"

"Just like that, Lieutenant."

"And Harvey had the gun in his hand?"

"If you think Harvey killed those two men, Lieutenant, you are a total idiot—"

"God save me! Harvey, get her the hell out of here! Get both of you the hell out of here. Get out of here and don't let me lay eyes on either of you again."

"You'll need us for witnesses," I said unhappily.

"God help me, I will." He stood up behind his desk. "Get out!"

We got out. We walked downstairs, and I said goodnight to Banniker, who was carrying a container of milk upstairs, and to the tired desk sergeant, and then we went out to the street. It was a cool but pleasant evening, and we walked west on 67th Street. I said to Lucille, "Funny, he didn't scare me so much this time. He could have thrown a murder rap at me."

"Harvey, who would ever think that you could kill two Texans?"

"Maybe someone would. How do you know?"

"Well, don't get angry at me just for that, Harvey."

"It's not for that. It's about Corsica. I hope Rothschild lays hands on him. I hope he rots in jail."

"Harvey, he saved your life."

"He's a lousy killer."

"Still, he saved your life. And mine. And Cynthia's. Anyway—what ever happened to Fats Coventry and the other two Texans?"

"They were taken away. Maybe in the same Fleetwood. Anyway, by the same crowd. Goddamn it, do you know why he was grinning?"

"I wish you wouldn't swear so much, Harvey."

"Just tell me, do you know why he was grinning?"

"Who?"

"The real Valento Corsica, when he told you to go ahead into the Rembrandt Room."

"What was he grinning about, Harvey?"

"Eighty-five thousand dollars. Eighty-five thousand dollars in traveler's checks—which I gave him as ransom for you and Cynthia."

"But we were in the next room, Harvey."

"You were indeed. He conned me. Me. Harvey Krim. Born and bred in this city, and a square cons me for eighty-five grand."

"Harvey, he was not a square. He's the head of the Mafia."

"Mafia? Weren't you telling me that there isn't any Mafia?" I turned left on Park Avenue now.

"Where are we going? Why don't we take a cab, Harvey?"

"It's right across the street. We're going to pay a call on Mr. E.C. Brandon."

"At this hour. It's one o'clock."

"They won't be sleeping. Remember, Kelly took her home just a little while ago."

"Harvey—are you sure?"

"I'm sure."

We went across Park Avenue and we entered 626 Park, and that same old crumb of a doorman barred my path.

"Get away," I said to him, "or I'll break you in two."

"I got to announce you. It's one in the morning."

"So announce us. We're going up."

We walked through to the elevator man, and I flashed my badge and told him we were going up. We went up.

Lucille whispered, "Harvey, you are wonderful when you act tough."

"Nuts."

"That's very good," she said. "That's good, solid slang."

I rang the bell and then I pounded on the Brandon door. The elevator man waited. "Beat it," I told him. Jonas Biddle, the butler, opened the door and demanded to know how I dared to make a row like that at one in the morning.

"Get lost," I said. "I want to see Brandon. Now."

"You can't see him. He's with his daughter."

"Where?"

"In the library."

"Biddle," I said, "I am going in there. Don't try to stop me. Call the cops if you want to, but if you do, you lose a job. Now where is the library?"

He pointed. I took Lucille by the arm, and we entered. It was a fine, high-class, expensive library, about five thousand dollars worth of leather upholstery and maybe twice as much in leather bindings. There was maybe ten, twelve thousand dollars of oriental rug on the floor, and on the walls, a Cezanne, a Monet, and a Mondrian. He was consistantly high-class about his pictures.

As we entered, Brandon was laying it on the line to Cynthia. "—and that finishes it," he was saying. "No more crazy benders, no more 'love it's wonderful,' no more computer dating, no more of those long-haired unwashed you have been seeing. From now on, I call the tune. Not one bloody nickel will you see—" He turned to me and snarled, "And just who the hell do you think you are, coming in here like this?"

"They're friends of mine!" Cynthia cried out.

"My name's Harvey Krim. This is Miss Lucille Dempsey."

"I remember. You're that insurance investigator. Well, the job's over. Get out!"

"No."

"Just what do you mean, Krim?"

"I mean my job's not over. Not at all."

"No?" He fixed his steely gaze on me, squared his already square jaw and said, "I've got news for you, Krim. Your job is very much over. Because I intend to see to it that you get fired. Push this one step further, and I will also see to it that you never work in this town again."

[184]

"Oh?"

"And people will tell you I am a man of my word, Krim."

I walked around the big mahogany desk, sat down in E.C.'s chair, took out my memo pad and wrote, "Fats Coventry told me who his client was. I have it on tape. I paid eight-five grand ransom for your daughter. I want a check for the same. Now." Then I folded the slip of paper and handed it to him. He started to crumple it, almost as a reflex action.

"Read it first, E.C.," I snapped at him.

He backed away from us, opened the paper and read it. Then he looked at me. Then he looked at Lucille and his daughter. Then he looked at me again. Then he read the slip of paper again—more slowly now. Then he looked at me a third time, and then he read what I had written for a third time. His face flushed at first; then it turned a shade of purple; then it became white. He was very pale now, and he looked very deadly indeed.

"Do they know anything about this?" he asked, nodding at his daughter and Lucille.

"No."

"Do you intend to tell them?"

"No."

"Why not?"

"I cultivate my own garden."

"Don't break your word to me, Krim. I'm not soft."

"Don't break your word to me, E.C."

"Where did you get it to begin with?" he demanded.

"From the company."

"And where does it go?"

"Back to them."

"My check?"

"Cash. I cash it first. Tomorrow morning."

[185]

"How do I know?"

"You don't."

We examined each other for a moment or two; then I got up and he took my place behind the desk. The girls were across the room. I stood over him and watched him write a check, payable to cash, for eighty-five thousand dollars. He folded it over and gave it to me, and I put it carefully in my wallet.

"Tell the bank to honor it," I said. "I'll cash it at ten tomorrow morning."

"Whatever is going on here," Cynthia said, "I am going with you two tonight."

"You don't have to," I told her.

"What do you mean? How do you know? Do you know what it means to live with him?"

"It's going to be easy to live with him now," I said. "Don't you agree with me, E.C.?"

He stared at me without replying.

"How?" Cynthia demanded.

"Nothing very special, but from now on, Cynthia, you will be a person in your own home. You will come and go as you please, and he will not question your coming and going. He will furnish you with an adequate allowance, and since this is your home, you can bring any friends you wish to bring right here. He will get off your back, once and for all."

Both Cynthia and Lucille were staring at me dumbly now.

"Am I right, E.C.?"

"You're doing the talking, Krim."

"I want you to say it to her, E.C. 'Krim is right'—just say that to her."

It was a hard one to swallow and regurgitate, but he managed it.

"Krim is right," he said.

"So if it happens otherwise, let me know, Cynthia. Just let me know. I'm in the phone book. Just telephone and let me know."

Still Cynthia was speechless.

"Go to bed now, kid," I told her.

She went to the door, paused, turned to us and said, "Good night, Harvey. Good night, Lucille." Then she stared at her father for a long moment. "Good night," she said to him. Then she left.

"Then this is the end of it?" Brandon asked me.

"I hope so."

He still sat behind his desk, staring at me. I glanced at Lucille, caught her eye, and motioned to the door. We went out. The butler let us out of the apartment, and downstairs Clapp said to me, "Make trouble somewhere else, shamus. Leave this house alone for a while."

"He called you shamus, Harvey," Lucille said excitedly as we walked down Park.

"He watches television."

"You were really angry, weren't you, Harvey?"

"I have been everyone's patsy. For a whole week now, I have been everybody's patsy. I'm tired of it."

"Mine, Harvey?"

"Not yours," I said.

"Thank heavens, Harvey. And that check was for eighty-five thousand dollars, wasn't it?"

"Your guess is as good as mine."

"Oh, Harvey, are you going to keep on talking like a private eye? I'm not sure I could take it for more than a day. And it was eighty-five thousand. That's terribly exciting, Harvey—but now that dreadful vice-president of your company—Homer Smedly, wasn't that his name?—well, he won't read you out of the human race at all because you'll cash the check in the morning and bring him the cash. That's terribly clever."

I shrugged.

"But you must have had something awful on E.C. Brandon to make him do it. He's supposed to be the chintziest man in town. What did you have on him, Harvey?"

"Nothing."

"Harvey, do you know what I think?"

"I don't want to know," I said.

"Harvey, I think he's the one who set up the whole thing— the whole crazy idea of stealing the Rembrandt. He's absolutely crazy, and it's just the kind of thing he would do. I'm right, aren't I, Harvey?"

"You're wrong and you're a nut," I said.

I got a cab then, and in the cab I kissed her. It was nothing I thought about. It was just something I wanted to do, and I did it, and then she said plaintively, "I must go back to work tomorrow, Harvey. It's been such fun."

I nodded gratefully.

"But we could have breakfast?"

"I got to be at the bank."

"Lunch?"

"All right," I agreed. "Lunch. At the Gotham. How about that?"

"Harvey Krim, last of the big spenders," she sighed sleepily.

I was half-asleep myself when I entered my apartment, and the telephone was ringing. I picked it up, and Homer Smedly's nasal voice said,

"About time you got in, Harvey. I see by the morning papers that you're a sort of hero. We like that. We like heroes working for the company. But you know what we like better?"

"Eighty-five grand," I said.

"Good thinking, Harvey."

"I'll bring you the cash in the morning."

"We'll take a check, Harvey."

"I prefer cash."

"Very well. Sleep tight. We'll be waiting."

"Good night," I said.